ALL CHICKENS MUST DIE

A

DETECTIVE

BENJAMIN WADE

MYSTERY

SCOTT DENNIS PARKER

QUADRANT FICTION STUDIO

2016

All Chickens Must Die

A Detective Benjamin Wade Mystery

ISBN-13: 978-0692638378
ISBN-10: 0692638377

Cover design by Scott Dennis Parker
Cover Photos:
Top: Peepo
Bottom: decisiveimages

www.ScottDennisParker.com

Give feedback on the book at:

scott@scottdennisparker.com

Twitter: @sdparker7

Second Edition

Printed in the U.S.A

NIGHTTIME INTRUDER!

I sat up, the springs of the couch creaking under my weight. It was then that I realized I was still dressed. I glanced at my watch. Too dark to see. I moved it so that the light from the streetlamp streaming through my blinds caught the hands on my watch. Three in the morning. Sheesh. When was the last time I was awake at that time of night?

I don't know about you, but I can tell when another person is in the same room even if I can't see anyone. As I sat there on my couch, ready to go to the kitchen, I felt the presence of someone. I couldn't explain how, but I did. Trepidation started to warp my mind. It was the middle of the night. Perhaps I was just imagining it. Perhaps there really wasn't anybody in my house.

Then again, I also thought I had closed the Venetian blind on my east window.

I tensed. The fog of fatigue evaporated. The click I heard must have been the click of the window lock. But if that was the case, then the intruder would have been outside, right? How in the world could the window latch have been opened from the outside?

It was then that I turned my eyes to the door. It was closed. I knew that because there was no light coming from around the frame. Additionally, it was in deep shadow so most things, including my hat rack, were practically in the dark.

But there was a shape standing in front of the door that didn't belong. The shape was a man. I could barely make out the outline, but it was distinctive enough.

There were no available weapons near at hand. My gun was in my bedroom. Lot of good it did me there. The question now was: would he let me get to the kitchen and get a knife? Chances were not good in that regard.

The alternative was simple: rush him and get the upper hand. The ache in my head made me wish I hadn't partaken of two shots of rye. I needed more sleep. But I needed to have that intruder out of my house more.

I stood and wobbled a moment. Were I a better actor, I could have thrown in some histrionics, making it appear I was more far gone than I truly was. Maybe throw my arms up.

I think he sensed he was made. I turned to the kitchen. He rushed me. Damn, he was fast.

For my family who puts up with me...

CHAPTER ONE

Do you know how embarrassing it is to be a private eye without a secretary? It means that every potential client sees you sitting in the outer office, typing your own reports and notes, and not in your main office with your feet on the desk, whiling away a hot summer's day looking at the Houston skyline. It would also have meant that clients such as Elmer Smith and his chicken problems would have been turned away and I never would have learned that a secret society existed here in Houston that had, as its one rule, the obligation to avenge any wrong done to any member, real or imagined.

Why I didn't just type my reports in my own office, I'll never know. I think, honestly, I wanted to convey the impression that I did, indeed, have a secretary. I didn't have one—yet—but I was actively looking for one. I had placed a classified ad in all the local papers and I had been interviewing many of the candidates over a few weeks. I found the decision to be extraordinarily difficult. I wanted the perfect combination of beauty and ability. To date, that type of woman hadn't walked in my door.

That didn't stop other types of women from waltzing in and looking for a job. This was May 1940 and the effects of the Depression still permeated the economy. It made me feel a little bad when I had to turn away a few applicants because they were not quite the type I was looking for. If you had put a gun to my head, I'd have admitted that the way a woman looked was pretty important. I'm running a small business and the first thing clients see is the secretary. She needs to be a knockout.

Martha Weber was sitting in the interview chair when Mr. Smith rang the front bell. I'd faced men with guns, but for some reason, that day I didn't want to face a potential client without a secretary.

"You want to make five bucks?" I said.

Martha looked at me with wariness. "What do I have to do?"

"Pretend to be my secretary."

She frowned. "So, I have the job?"

"No, but I'd like you to pretend to be my secretary for that potential client out there."

"Why don't I have the job?"

I winced. That was an argument best discussed among other men. Only they could understand the importance of an attractive secretary for private-eye business. Martha had the typing skills in spades. But her looks were on the homely side. She looked like she belonged in a school or public library, not at the receptionist/typist for a private investigator firm.

"I have a few other applicants, and I need to give them

a chance, you know?"

"I'm a great typist. I can even do some field work, if you need it. Did I tell you I'm pretty good with a gun?" She said the last with a bit more emphasis than was necessary.

The doorbell rang again. Work wasn't flowing as I would have liked. I was in a dire position of having to take almost everything that came through the door. I desperately didn't want any potential clients to leave.

I gave her a double take. "Double my offer. Ten dollars."

Martha looked at me sidelong. "You really got it?"

Sure, I just won't get any gas for a week. "I'll get the client to make a down payment."

"You'd better." She rose from her chair. "I'll be right back, Mr. Wade." She winked at me and sashayed out of my office. Seeing her from behind, I had second thoughts about doing this. What if she blew it?

Through the closed door, I heard soft murmuring then Martha's shape through the frosted glass door. Didn't every private eye have doors with frosted glass?

The door cracked and Martha stuck her head in. "Mr. Wade, there are two gentlemen here to see you."

Two gentlemen? I rarely got pairs of potential clients. "Please send them in..." I paused and my eyes raced across my desk until I found her file. "Miss Weber."

She narrowed her eyes. I shrugged. I cinched up my tie and sat up straighter in my chair.

The first man who walked in I didn't recognize. He wore, of all things, denim overalls. The hat he held in his hands looked nicer than his entire wardrobe, his pressed shirt notwithstanding. I pegged him for a farmer and quickly dreaded needing to take any job to pay the rent. I wasn't up for some sort of cow theft.

The second man, on the other hand, I knew. Burt Haldeman was a lawyer, a shyster if you ask me. He was the kind of man who used his size and bulk to get his way when his words failed him. Half the time, that's what happened. His tie only reached halfway down his gut. Not flattering, but his looks were enough to land a semi-slob like me in Life magazine.

I stood and came around my desk, extending my hand to the lawyer. "Burt, how you doing? What brings you in my door?"

"Good to see you again, Wade," Haldeman said. "I see you landed on your feet after that little incident."

I cleared my throat. "Sure did." I pivoted and introduced myself to the farmer.

He took my hand, his leathery, hard skin felt like some sort of moving beef jerky. "Elmer Smith." He was looking around, clearly out of his element.

"Please, gentlemen, have a seat." I indicated the two chairs opposite my desk. To Martha, I said, "Thank you, Miss Weber. That will be all." She rubbed her thumb and index finger together in the universal sign of money.

With their backs to her, Haldeman and Smith were unable to see Martha. I smiled and nodded once, then gestured her out.

I sat and leaned my elbows on the desk. "What brings you into my office?"

"Chickens," Smith said.

I looked to Haldeman for confirmation. He nodded in assent.

"Chickens," I said. "I can't say I've ever had a case involving chickens."

"Judging from how long you've been doing this little job," Haldeman said, "I'd have to agree with you. But, nonetheless, we are here on account of chickens." He reached into his suit and pulled out a pack of cigarettes. He shook one out, put it between his lips, and lit up. "Tell him, Elmer."

The farmer cleared his throat. I got the impression he wasn't used to speaking in public. "Well, you see, Mr. Wade, the agriculture man, the health inspector man, wants to condemn all my chickens and kill'em all."

I waited for additional details. Smith, his mouth a thin line with almost no upper lip, sat there as if he had just spoken a fact, like the color of the sky or the humidity level in town that day. Turning to Haldeman, I raised my eyebrows. "Burt?"

Haldeman smiled. "It's true. Mr. Smith's entire brood of chickens has been declared unsanitary by the health inspector. They're scheduled to be slaughtered in the next few days. I got Judge Briscoe to put a temporary injunction on the slaughter, but we're running outta time."

"I'm still not seeing where I come in."

Smith frowned. "Ain't it obvious? I need you to investigate that bastard inspector and figure out why he's trying to kill my livelihood."

CHAPTER TWO

I did my best to keep my mouth closed, concentrating hard to breathe through my nose and act like what I just heard was something you heard every day, like the weather or the news the Nazis had invaded another country.

"Why don't you tell me what's been going on, Mr. Smith?" I even prompted the speech by getting out a yellow legal pad. I held my pen poised over it, ready to write down notes.

"Okay," Smith said, "I can do that. You takin' notes?"

Opting not to restate the obvious, I merely nodded. "Ready when you are."

"Well, it was a few weeks ago and there was a ruckus at my chicken farm."

"Where's your farm?"

"West of here, out past the bayou."

"What kind of 'ruckus' did you hear?" I was thinking a wolf, but kept my options open.

"You know, I didn't rightly know what it was. One night, about two, maybe three weeks ago, I'm sitting in my house and I hear the sound of cars. They was coming to a stop, kinda hurry like, you know, like they was speeding."

"Is that unusual? Do you live near roads?"

"Course I live near roads. They take me to market. Anyways, I hear cars stopping and tires screeching. I'm not sure what's going on so I head on outta the house to get a look around, you know?"

I nodded. I shook out a cigarette. This was going to take a while.

"I hear something in my barn and chicken coop so I make my way over there. That's when I hear footsteps."

"Running or walking?"

"Beg pardon?"

"The sounds the feet were making, did they sound like they were walking or running?"

"What difference does that make?"

"A lot actually." I inhaled a huge lungful of smoke and blew a smoke ring up towards the ceiling. "If it's running, then someone is running away from something."

"Or running towards something," Haldeman said.

"Perhaps," I said, "but unless there was a wreck or some sort of bad accident where folks ran toward it to get a look-see or to help, chances were the footsteps were running away from something. Any idea what it might be?"

"Not really," Smith said, "but the police would know.

They was the ones chasing some guy through my chicken coop."

Great, I thought. The police. Not exactly my favorite group of citizens, not since I got booted off the force and had to fend for myself as a civilian without a badge and the power that went with it.

Aloud, I said, "You file a police report for this—what theft? What did this health inspector steal?"

"He ain't steal nothing. He weren't there the night of the disturbance. He came afterwards and told me that all my chickens would have to be kilt in order to meet his health demands. On the night of the chase, only them police came around. Said they were chasing some hoodlum was speeding."

Odd, I thought. The police don't usually chase speeders. Then again, speeders don't usually ditch their cars and hoof it.

I paused halfway through an inhale. "Okay, so let me get this straight. You have a disturbance at your farm, police show up chasing someone on foot. You live far enough away, I assume, that anyone who comes by your house probably has to drive out there, right?"

"Yeah."

"Did you hear the other car?"

Smith stared at the ceiling, lost in thought. A little tip of his tongue actually stuck out. I thought I was watching a Bugs Bunny cartoon in real life.

"Come to think of it, I think I might've."

"Did the cops not think to ask that question?"

"No, I don't reckon so. I ain't all in the country, you know. I'm only part way in the country. There's a few roads that go past my land, pretty much on all sides."

"Who lives around you? Anyone famous or rich? Any way someone could have mistaken your house for some larger house nearby?"

"On the west side, there's just another farm. On the east side, acrost the bayou, there's a bunch of rich sons of bitches. They live in a neighborhood nearby. New houses gone up in '39."

I frowned. "Cops look over your land and property to determine if anything was stolen?"

"Yeah."

"Anything?" It was like pulling teeth to get him to talk.

"No."

Pass the pliers. I got another tooth. "You file a police report?"

"No. Didn't seem to be a crime."

I glanced at the lawyer. Haldeman was the kind of shyster that gave lawyers a bad name. If there wasn't a crime committed, he'd invent one. "Counselor?"

"No crime or police report. Nothing out of the ordinary until the health inspector."

I had to stifle a chuckle. Haldeman spoke with such authority you would've thought having the cops show up on your land was a routine occurrence. "I'll check with HPD, see if they can tell me what they were doing that night. Back to this health inspector you want me to follow. What was his name again?"

"Brad Teague." Haldeman cut off his client just as he was about to speak. "He works at the local branch of the Texas Animal Health Commission. He's the one who is ordering all of my client's chickens to be slaughtered."

"Teague give a reason?"

"Said it was to prevent some sort of infectious disease. He used some sort of fancy Latin words to tell me what it was, but it's all bunk. I keep that coop clean and free of all pests. He ain't got no claim, but he says he does." The farmer nodded to Haldeman. "That's why I hired this here lawyer."

Haldeman had the gall to bow from the neck.

Seeing as I didn't have many prospects at the moment and, if I was going to hire a secretary, I'd need some capital, I said, "I'll take the job." I made a show of opening up my calendar, ensuring the blank pages were well hidden from Haldeman. "I'll need a down payment of twenty-five percent plus fifty for expenses."

Smith didn't bat an eye. He pulled out his wallet and slid a small pile of cash across the desk to me. "I hope that's enough, Mr. Wade. I had to open my safe deposit box."

And then the guilt pang hit my gut. Fleeting though it was, I still felt it. Of course, it didn't stop my fingers from handling the cash and giving it a quick count. One hundred even. Good enough.

"Thank you, Mr. Smith." I stood and offered him my hand. "I'll provide you with weekly reports."

"That's not good enough." Haldeman stood as well. "We've only got five more days until the injunction runs out. We're going to need answers fast."

I stifled the scowl threatening to crease my face. I didn't like being told what to do in my own office.

Smith's countenance changed. Gone was the weathered farmer who spent all his days outside and the skin to prove it. He relaxed a bit. His eyes grew softer. "Mr. Wade, I'm desperate. My chickens are all my wife and I have. They've kept us out of the soup lines all during this Depression. If they're killed, we'll lose our farm, especially since them damn rich folks keep taking all the farmers' land."

Great, I thought. No pressure.

Inwardly, I chastened myself. Sure, I didn't have a lot of dough, but I had more than Smith. I shook Smith's hand. "I'll start right away."

CHAPTER THREE

The local branch of the Texas Animal Health Commission (TAHC) in Houston was located in one of the more modern buildings constructed with New Deal money. The light tan bricks and green-tinted glass certainly gave off that Art Deco flavor so dearly loved by scores of architects since about 1922. I didn't mind it so much in movie theaters or restaurants, but office buildings were a different animal.

The office was situated in the middle of a block of other similarly built office buildings in the shadow of downtown. I had to circle the block before I found a parking space. I walked past an all-night diner that was making the transition from breakfast to lunch. Office workers and construction guys were already milling about, smoking cigarettes, shooting the breeze, or reading the paper bought from the nearby newsstand. Overhead, the latest Doc Savage and The Shadow pulp magazines were hanging by strings. I loved the pulps. Dime Detective sat on my night table back home.

I opened the door to the TAHC and went inside. It was quiet, with only a couple of people waiting off to the side. Two receptionists sat behind desks. One was a brunette, hair pulled back all neat and tidy. Her dress was an off-green with a small string of pearls around her neck. The other was a redhead, more the darker kind that only flashed red when the light hit her hair just right. Her work attire consisted of a beige dress with a turquoise necklace. There was something familiar about the redhead, but I couldn't place her.

The redhead was helping another customer, so I sauntered over to the brunette.

"Can I help you?" Her blue eyes dazzled me.

"Yes, I'm here to see Brad Teague."

"Can I ask in what regard you want to see Mr. Teague?"

"You can ask," I said, giving levity to the comment. It didn't fly. I dropped the charm attack. "I'd like to talk with him about some chickens. My name's Wade." I didn't want to flash my credentials so soon in case she might tip off her boss.

There was something in the way she looked at me that I didn't like. Nonetheless, she picked up the receiver and spoke into it. The conversation went on longer that I expected. It was as if she was trying to convince him to see me. In the end, she won.

"Mr. Teague will see you now."

I thanked her, keeping eye contact a few seconds too long. She looked away first. She rose and led me back to a short hallway that ended with a corner office. Gently rapping on the door, she opened the door and walked in.

"Mr. Teague, this is Mr. Wade. He's here to talk about some chickens."

Brad Teague looked up from whatever he was writing. He peered at us through thick lenses that made his eyes look as big as marbles. I felt the sudden urge to extend two fingers and ask how many. I refrained. I didn't think he'd pass. His brown suit was rumpled and there was a ring of sweat around his collar.

"Thank you, Clara." Teague stood behind his desk and waited for me to approach. I was more interested in the fact that I now knew the name of the receptionist.

Clara lowered her eyes and head and scurried out of the room. I walked over and shook Teague's hand. Like the rest of him, his palm was sweaty and clammy. I wanted to wipe my hand. Instead I sat in one of the chairs opposite the desk which, naturally, gave me the chance to wipe my palm on my trousers.

Teague sat behind his desk and steepled his fingers. "Mr. Wade, how can I help you?"

I glanced around the room, taking in the sparse interior design. File cabinets lined one wall, a map of Texas hung on another, a picture frame faced Teague. Family?

"Morning, Mr. Teague. I was wondering what you can tell me about Elmer Smith." I liked starting off interviews with a bang. It gave me a chance to assess the other person.

Teague didn't disappoint. He cleared his throat and

discovered new meaning in his desk pad. "Elmer Smith," he said, delaying his answer. "I may have to look that one up. We get so many requests every week."

I hooked a thumb over my shoulder to the lobby. "You aren't busy now. I waltzed right in like I owned the place."

Teague grinned nervously, pulling his cuffs from under his blazer. "Right. It's an off day."

"Off day versus your usual hectic schedule?"

"Why do you want to know about"—he paused as if he had forgotten the name; he was a bad actor—"Elmer Smith?"

Sometimes it pays to be up front with a person of interest. I did that all the time when I was a cop. Granted, in those days, I had the badge to back me up. Nowadays, when people learn I'm a private investigator, they tend to clam up and stop talking to me. Teague was already close to that, so I invented a story on the spot.

"I run a chicken farm down in Fort Bend County and I heard through the grapevine that Smith got in some hot water with y'all. There's a part of me that wants to gloat, but there's another part of me that wants to make sure my flock doesn't fall prey to what he's into. Can you let me know why he's on your slaughter list?"

Teague's face twitched. He reached to the pack of Camels sitting on his desk and inched one out. He put fire to it and I got to see his shaking fingers. I think I hit a nerve.

I pressed him. "I got a livelihood to consider. I was in town to see a banker and thought I'd swing by, have a little meeting with you." I took out my notebook, wondering if a real farmer would do such a thing. "So, what is it?"

The string of Latin-sounding names that came out of his mouth seemed to be one of those times when a mark starts piling on highfaluting words to hide the truth. I did the phonic spelling thing and wrote down words that sounded like the words he spoke. I'd have to check them later for any grain of truth.

"I'm sorry," I said, "but my Latin or whatever language you just spoke is rusty. Can you say it again, in English?"

Teague cleared his throat. "Mr. Smith's chickens all are suffering from an ailment that has only one guarantee of success: kill all the chickens."

"When's this going to take place?"

Teague checked his calendar. "It was already supposed to have happened last week, but the court issued a temporary halt and we're waiting."

I help up a finger. "If his chickens posed an imminent threat to his life and those of the chickens in the area, what judge would grant that kind of order?"

Holding up his cigarette, Teague shrugged.

"Who talked to the court?"

"Smith himself and his no-good lawyer."

"Why's his lawyer trying to stop it?"

"The chickens are Smith's livelihood, same as you. Wouldn't you try to stop the wholesale slaughter of your entire flock?"

I tilted my head in affirmation. "That I would. And I'd use all available means at my disposal. You know which judge granted the injunction?"

"Fellow by the name of Briscoe. He's one of them judges who thinks everything FDR does is a gift from heaven. The man's just the president. He ain't Jesus or anything."

I decided to keep him talking. "What do you think about the war? Think we'll stay out of it?"

"I damn sure hope so," Teague said. "France'll pull through fine. They got themselves a damn good army. And that Maginot Line will stop the Germans in their tracks. This thing'll be over way before they need us in there. Just as well, too. We ain't ready."

"Ready for war, you mean?"

"Of course. We ain't ready. Don't mean we can't get ready."

"What about Roosevelt? Think he'll run for a third term?"

"Probably. Who do the Democrats have in reserve?"

"No one good enough, that's for sure. So, this Judge Briscoe, he's a New Dealer?"

"Yup." In the course of the conversation, he started to talk more freely and some of his trepidation left him.

"Who was the one who reported the contamination?"

"Beg pardon?"

"The disease or whatever's afflicting the chickens over at Smith's farm, who brought it to y'all's attention?"

Whatever joviality Teague had let into his system vanished without a trace. "Why is that important to your chickens and farm?"

I shrugged. "Just want to know. In case it's one of those vegetarians who think killing all animals is bad. I'd hate to think one of them got you to declare his chickens bad. Y'all got science to back that up?"

"Of course we have science," Teague snapped. He stubbed out his cigarette in the glass ashtray. He narrowed his eyes. "You said you live in Fort Bend County. I didn't catch your name."

I stood. "It's Wade. Thanks for your time. I'll see myself out."

CHAPTER FOUR

I ducked out of Teague's office and closed the door. From inside, I heard the sound of his chair scraping on wood. To my left was the lobby. To the right was the back door, I hoped. I went right.

A couple of more turns and I found myself in the break room. The smell of old coffee filled the air. There was a woman standing next to the coffee pot pouring herself a cup. It took me a moment to realize it was the receptionist who I had spoken to when I first got here. What was her name? Clara.

"You're not supposed to be back here," Clara said.

"I know. I'm just finding my way out without having your boss finding me."

"Why?" She put the coffee pot back on the burner.

"I'm not in the mood to answer any of his questions about me."

"Aren't you just a farmer?" The slight smile turned her lips up and a certain levity came into her eyes.

"Not really." I wasn't sure if I should tip her off to who I was. For all I knew, she and Teague might've been an item. On the other hand, she might be able to give me a little insight into why Teague was ordering the slaughter.

I closed the door behind me. "The order to kill a flock of chickens. How do y'all usually get the tip that something's amiss?"

Clara looked at me with unreadable eyes. She pursed her lips, trying to figure out something, probably like why I was asking a question like that. "Why do you want to know?"

I put my ear to the door and heard movement down the hall. Time to leave. I scanned the room for another door. Finding it, I made my way across the break room. I put my hand on the knob and turned back to Clara.

I weighed again the possibility that she was actually working with Teague to flush me out, but discarded that idea almost as soon as I thought it. She just didn't seem the type.

"My name's Wade. I'm a private investigator. I'm looking into Teague and the animal commission to determine why Elmer Smith's chickens are scheduled for slaughter. You know anything about that?"

At the mention of my profession, her countenance changed completely. Her eyes widened and her mouth dropped open.

"Can I talk to you?" she asked.

I nodded to the door. "No time for that now."

"Somewhere else then?"

I pursed my lips. She wanted to spill something. Might as well find out what. "Sure."

"I have lunch at eleven thirty. Can you meet me at Jake's Diner on Washington?"

"Sure." Now it was my turn to ask why and I did.

"Because I think someone is following me."

CHAPTER FIVE

Jake's Diner on Washington was one of those places where a man can get just about anything his heart craves at pretty much any time of day. I knew it well, but considered it an odd choice for Clara to suggest until I reckoned she didn't want to be seen. Taking a cue, I homesteaded on a booth near the back with little access to the side windows. At eleven forty, she breezed into the joint, looking a little nervous as she scanned the room. I held up my hand and she found me.

She slid into the booth opposite. Again, she looked over her shoulder and around the room.

"Who are you hiding from?"

"I wanted to make sure I wasn't followed."

I scanned the wall of windows behind her, seeing if there were any loiterers around. Other than a newsstand and a crowded bus stop, no one was watching for her.

I extended my hand. "Benjamin Wade."

She shook my hand, her delicate fingers almost tickling my skin. "Clara Milbanks."

"What makes you think someone's following you?"

Before she could answer, the waitress arrived. "What can I get y'all?"

I had already reviewed the menu before Clara arrived, but I did it again to give her time to look. "I'll have the club sandwich and coffee. Whatever she wants, it's on me."

Clara smiled and put the menu down. "I'll have a chicken salad sandwich and iced tea."

The waitress put her pencil behind her ear and moved back to the kitchen to place our order.

"Okay." I leaned on my elbows and clasped my hands together. "What happened?"

"Are you really a private investigator?"

I pulled out my license and showed her. "How much do you know about the Smith case?"

"We get to know most cases that come through the office. I know the Smith one because it's the only one that has a court injunction against it."

"That doesn't happen too often?"

"Almost never."

"You know who contacted y'all, tipped off the commission about the chickens?"

The waitress brought our drinks and food. You have to give it up to diners like Jake's: the service is quick and hearty if a little greasy.

Around a mouthful of chicken salad, Clara said, "That's actually why I wanted to meet you. I wasn't sure where I could turn for help."

"Help with what?"

"Help in determining why this guy is following me."

I scowled. "Why would someone do that?"

"Because of what I heard about Mr. Smith."

"What did you hear?"

"About a week ago, a man I had never seen came into the office. I remembered him because he looked out of place by the way he dressed. Kinda like you in a way, but he dressed nicer, if you don't mind me saying so."

"Not at all. I tend to dress medium most of the time. You ought to see me when I'm playing ball."

She leaned in closer to me. "Here's the thing: I wasn't supposed to be there. It was Danny's turn to stay late, but she couldn't do it, so I volunteered for her."

"Who's Danny?"

"Danielle Bowie. The other secretary you saw in the main office."

I put that name with the image of the redhead. They seemed to go together.

"Okay. Y'all staying late, that a regular thing?"

"Usually once a week, one of us stays late and works with some of the inspectors on outstanding cases. You wouldn't believe how far behind we get when we're neck-deep in all the inspections."

"I can imagine. Most of those cases come into your office how?"

"Random inspections. Or regularly scheduled ones. We do both."

"So, if a farmer knows you always come on the fifteenth of a month, he can, I assume, always be ready for you?"

"Theoretically, yes. Which is why we do spot inspections. Catch them off-guard if they are not keeping their farms and animals clean."

"But what about tip offs? You get a lot of them?"

"We get some."

"You obliged to follow them all up?"

"Usually, yes."

"You always send out an investigator?"

"Yes."

"Any advance warning?"

"Not usually, no."

"Tip offs ever come from disgruntled rivals?"

"From time to time."

"You write them off as frivolous or do you have to investigate?"

"We always investigate. It's the law."

"You ever get tip-offs you know are bogus?"

She paused, thinking. "Sometimes. The accused, just like in a real court, gets to defend himself. He has to prove his innocence, however. That's a bit of a change over the typical court system."

I sipped my coffee and took more bites out of my sandwich. The bacon had just the right amount of crispy and chewy. Jake's is one of the few places that sprinkle brown sugar over cooking bacon. The flavor is sublime.

I couldn't help noticing the way she ate her food and drank her tea. It was all dainty. She wiped the corners of her mouth with her napkin. Again, I got the sudden realization she must be truly upset to show up in a greasy spoon.

"Back to what you heard. Tell me about it."

She drank off some of her tea and wiped her mouth. How'd she do that and still keep her lipstick in place?

"So, last week, I was working in Danny's place. She had to take her elderly mother to the pharmacy and she needed to swap days with me. We did, no big deal, and I saw her off.

I pulled out my notebook and opened to a blank page.

"It was just after closing time when the man I told you about showed up in the office. He wore a very nice blue suit and a yellow tie. He had one interesting thing: a tie clip in the shape of a sideways eight."

"A sideways eight?"

"Yeah, you know, a figure eight but on its side. Give me your pen."

I did as instructed and she drew the image on a napkin.

"Oh, that's the infinity symbol."

"Maybe," she said, "but it didn't actually meet at the middle. There was some space in there. Not sure why."

"So this guy wearing an infinity tie clip comes to your office and what?"

"He met with Mr. Teague. But before that, the new man gave me a weird look. The first thing that was weird was when he saw me. He looked surprised. It was like he was expecting someone else."

"Who?"

"Danielle."

I took my pen back and recorded that fact. "What did this guy do when he found out you weren't Danielle?"

She paused, thinking. "He gave me a weird look, like the look you give someone who is in the wrong place. It was really strange."

She finished off her sandwich and washed it down with the last of her tea. I took the opportunity to send the last mouthful of my sandwich down my gullet. I signaled the waitress for more coffee and tea, then folded my hands and leaned on my elbows.

"So this man went into Mr. Teague's office. They closed the door, but the walls are thin and I was the only other person in the building. I could hear my own breath if I wanted to. It was no big thing to hear when the heated voices starting to yell at each other."

"What did they say?"

"Now, even though the walls are thin, I couldn't hear every word. One thing the man kept saying was 'It's your obligation to do this.' He said it more than once."

"Any clue what that meant?"

She shook her head. "Not at all, but Teague got pretty worked up over it. He yelled back something like, 'but that's illegal. The government will know what I've done if they investigate."

I wrote that down in my notebook. "Any idea what he was talking about?"

"I'm not sure, but it was the next day when Mr. Teague ordered the slaughter of Mr. Smith's chickens."

I gazed at her. Now we were getting somewhere. "Okay, so this mystery man comes to your office after hours, has a fight with Teague, and the next day, Teague orders the slaughter?

She nodded and looked out the window at the noontime sun beating down on the pavement. The heat shimmered off the street. "Mr. Teague pulled me aside two days after that and asked if I had heard anything. I was scared. Of course I heard everything, or the stuff that mattered most. But I couldn't say anything or he'd fire me. Or worse."

"This guy who's following you. Same mystery man who came to the office late?"

"No." She clinked the ice cubes in the glass. "Last Friday night, Danny and I met up after work to go to a dance hall."

"Y'all often go out together?"

"From time to time. It's not odd, but the timing was. You see, we hadn't gone out for a month or two. Then, suddenly, she suggests Friday night. I didn't have anything to do so I agreed. There's a dance hall down on Bell Avenue. You know the one?"

I nodded. It had been a while since I took a lady out on the town, but I knew the place. Not only did traveling big bands come and play at the Travis Dance Hall, but a good number of Texas swing bands played there, too.

"We were there an hour and this man shows up at our table."

"What'd he look like?"

She shrugged. "He was taller than you by a few inches, dark hair, no mustache, dressed nicely. The thing I noticed about him was his hands. They were huge."

"'Huge' as in long or 'huge' as in thick?"

"A little of both. He introduced himself as Amos Peete and he asked me to dance." She stopped as if letting the gravity of that statement rest on me.

I didn't get the meaning so I asked her about it.

"Mr. Wade, I know I'm not a looker, and Danny's ten times the lady I am, so it was odd to have him come over and ask me to dance."

I smiled. "Maybe he saw your eyes. They're quite radiant."

A blush crept across her face and I used the moment to signal the waitress for more drinks and the check. "All I'm saying," I reassured her, "is that this Peete guy might've just found you more attractive than your friend. So, you dance with him. What makes you think he's out to get you?"

The waitress came and poured more coffee and tea. Clara stirred in sugar and gave me a stare. "While we danced, we made small talk like new couples always do. When the song was over, he insisted we dance again. It was a ballad so we had more time to talk. He went on and on about my looks and how beautiful I was."

I had to agree with this Peete guy. Clara Milbanks might not have ever landed on the cover of a fashion magazine but she was far from unattractive. In fact, the more I sat across from her, the more I saw the beauty of her face, her hands, and the way she carried herself. Sure, she was telling me about some guy who she thought was trying to get her, but she was easily someone I wouldn't mind having on my arm.

I kept that little tidbit to myself. "Miss Milbanks, what makes you think Peete is out to get you?"

She sighed. "Two things. One was an offhand comment Mr. Teague made on Monday."

I frowned. "I thought we were talking about Peete."

"We are," she said, just a little too rushed, "but Mr. Teague plays into it. Early Monday morning, Mr. Teague casually mentions that it would be in my best interests to forget what I heard, if I heard anything. He said he'd hate to have to replace me in case I got into an accident."

I looked at her evenly, weighing the words. It was certainly a plausible non-threat that was, in fact, a threat. If it came up in court, he could deny he said it or, at worst, come across as a boss who was just wondering what might happen if Clara got hit by a bus. On the other hand, Teague was clearly threatening Clara to stay silent.

And just had just broken her silence. With me.

"I see what you mean." I shook out a cigarette from my pack of Camels and offered her one. She took one and I lit both with my Zippo. "Any comment like that since then?"

"No."

"And where does Peete fit into this?"

She shook her head and closed her eyes. "Maybe I'm just making too much of it."

"Tell me and I'll tell you if you're making too much of it."

"Well, I had never seen Mr. Peete at all until last Friday. Then, on Saturday, as I was at the grocery store, I bumped into him. We talked. One thing led to another and he asked me out that evening."

"And?"

"And we went out. We saw this new movie, Road to Singapore, with Bob Hope, Bing Crosby, and Dorothy Lamour. It was a gas. Afterwards, we went out for drinks. It was all very nice. He tried to kiss me as he dropped me off at home, but it was all awkward."

"I know you're getting somewhere but I don't see the problem."

"Well, I bumped into him again on Sunday. This time, at church."

I shrugged. "So, if I got this right, you see him first on Friday, you see him again on Saturday and y'all go out on a date, then you see him again on Sunday morning. Could it be that he's just smitten with you?"

Another minor blush tinted her face. "I suppose. But after church, we had lunch. He started asking a lot more particular questions about my daily life, where I got my hair done, what I did for fun besides dance. It got creepy.

So much so that I excused myself after the meal and went home. Late that afternoon, I took a stroll to my friend's house for bridge"—she paused, as if for effect—"and I saw him again along the way."

"You sure it was him?"

"Mr. Wade, I know what I saw. He was there, and he followed me. I'm sure of it."

"Was he there when you walked home?" I was beginning to see a pattern.

"I think so. Maybe he was better at hiding from me, but I certainly got the feeling I was being watched."

"And has it continued since then?"

She nodded. "I saw him getting his shoes shined just yesterday after work."

"He see you?"

"Sure. He said 'hello' and 'fancy meeting you here.'"

I glanced out the windows at the shoe shine right outside the diner. There were two men sitting in the chairs and three standing in line waiting. Of the three men, two were reading the newspaper. The third appeared to be looking directly at me.

I swept my eyes past him, hoping I appeared as nonchalant as possible. "Let me ask you a question. This Peete fellow, he wear a dark gray fedora? Have a face that's long in the chin with a dimple?"

The color that had pinked Clara's face vanished. She stared at me and started to turn around.

I reached out and clasped her hand. "Don't turn around. You might tip him off." I reached around and slipped my wallet from my pocket. I didn't want Peete to see me doing this for fear he'd book it. I slid a five-dollar bill out and placed it on the table. "Look, I know this is going to be awkward, but I need to have you go and pay for our lunch."

"Why?"

"Because I want him watching you while I slip out the back. And don't stare at him. Act like you've not seen him."

Clara swallowed. She nodded and gathered her purse.

"I'll call you later."

A partial smile returned to her face. "You're too kind, Mr. Wade. I think the outlook on my fate just got better."

She rose, covering my view for a moment. When she breezed up to the counter, I watched his gaze follow her. I slipped out of the booth and backed into the kitchen.

"Hey," a man wearing a greasy apron said, "you're not allowed back here."

I doffed my hat and smiled. "Just trying to avoid a jealous husband." Mollified, the man pointed to the back door. I opened it, hurried around the east side and peered around the corner. I saw the men standing in line at the shoe shine and I watched as Clara exited the front door. Sure enough, the man who had to be Peete followed her with his head. I crept up close to him, avoiding the other passersby.

His head did a double take back to the front door then to her walking toward her car.

"Right here," I said.

He whirled. I'll admit I wasn't ready for the swinging fist. His right came at me high. I ducked, but the bulk of his hand got me behind the ear. I saw stars and fell to one knee. Then I heard his footsteps hurry away.

"You okay, mister?" A man helped me up.

I shook my head to clear it. "Which way?"

The Good Samaritan and others pointed to a fleeing man. He was half a block away and seemed to be gaining speed. Even if I hadn't been groggy, I couldn't run that fast.

The shoe shine man gave me a look. "Shine your shoes, sir? They got scuffed."

I looked down. So they did. I shrugged. "Might as well," I muttered to myself. "Now I have two cases."

CHAPTER SIX

Even though I now had two cases, there was still the matter of the burglary near Smith's house. If there was anyone who might have a line on the police activity that occurred the previous week, it was my good friend Gordon Gardner. The man was an ace reporter for the Houston Post-Dispatch who got his big break on the same case I got mine: the search for Lillian Saxton's brother and the papers he smuggled out of Germany last month. I found the body. Gardner found the papers. He read them, but, under the influence of the Army and his editor, agreed never to utter a word about what he had read. Gardner kept to his word, even when he was writing at his big new desk as payment from his editor for his silence. Hey, silence has a price, right?

I strolled into the news room. The smell of ink, cigarette smoke, and coffee assaulted my nose. The click-clack of the typewriters made the room sound more like a huge machine than a place where men formed thoughts and wrote sentences. Perhaps it was only to keep pace with our rapidly moving world.

A few of the reporters gave me waves or nods. I had known a few of them from my time as a beat cop. Back then, we were on opposite sides and the relationship was more antagonistic than necessary. Some of those reporters had forgiven me. Others, not so much.

I started walking to the far corner where Gardner's big desk sat, then halted. Another guy was in the seat. What was his name? Flynn, I think. He looked up and our gazes met. He sneered. I rolled my eyes and tried to remember where Gardner sat now that he was demoted down to the society page. He still averred it was a demotion but he got to spend his working days with photographer Lucy Barnes, a stunning example of womanhood.

At the far corner, next to the window, sat Gardner. Stacks of papers lined the perimeter of his desk. A small pile of cigarettes moldered in the ashtray. The white coffee cup was stained inside and out. A cigarette hung from his lips, unlit. Perhaps he was just too busy to light it.

"How's it going?" I sat in the chair next to his desk.

Gardner looked up and took a puff on his cigarette. He frowned at the non-smoke, then took it out of his mouth and looked at it like it was some sort of defective machine. I flicked my Zippo and held the flame at the ready for him to light up. He did, then leaned back in his chair.

"How's it going, Wade? It's going blazes. The damn Nazis are invading western Europe, Norway's being lost by the Brits and the Frogs. The Nazis already invaded Belgium, Holland, Luxembourg, and France." He puffed and blew smoke out of his nose. "But the French should stop Hitler. It's what they got the Maginot line for, right? We got news reports coming in from all over. We're just trying to compile and get a handle on'em."

"So, not much. Anything local?"

"War coverage edges out lots of local news. We still have cow reports and the weather and whatever the governor is doing, but not much else. And, to top it all off, I get to sit on my ass and report about bigwigs and their damn parties. You know how infuriating it is to sit over here while everyone out there"—he gestured to the news room at large—"gets to cover real events?"

"You get to work with Lucy. Isn't that a nice reward?"

A smile cracked his face. "Yes, that is extremely nice. I've been to more highfalutin' parties since I got this assignment than the rest of my life put together. Having her on my arm, even in a professional context, is well worth it. But you didn't come here to chitchat about who's who. Why are you here?"

"I was wondering if your paper covered something from last week."

He raised an eyebrow. "Don't you read my paper?"

"Every day."

"Then you should know if whatever you're asking was in the paper."

"But that's the thing: I don't memorize everything I read, and I only got a new case this morning. Two actually."

Gardner sat up straighter. He enjoyed hearing the details of my cases. It helped him when he moonlighted as a writer of pulp stories. "Tell me."

"I got hired by a farmer to look into why the animal health department has scheduled his entire flock to be slaughtered."

Part of his enthusiasm vanished. "Really?"

"Really. But there's more."

"Hope so. Otherwise, you got the short end of the curiosity stick."

"Nice. The same night, there was some sort of police chase. The farmer, my client, says he saw the cops storm through his land looking for some sort of fugitive."

Gardner rubbed his hands together. "Now, we're talking. What'd this fugitive do?"

I held out my hands and shrugged. "That's why I'm here. Figured I'd get the real story first before I head over to HPD for the official police report."

Gardner stood and slapped me on the back. "See, you're finally thinking correctly. Not like you used to when you were a cop."

I shrugged again. "Who does your police beat?"

"Lorenzo Barr. He's a cub reporter, wet behind the ears, but he's got a knack for reading between the official lines."

"He here?"

"Let's go see him."

***

Lorenzo Barr was that squirrelly type of man who was too small in stature to match his likely vivid imagination. Around his desk were photos, cut from magazines and newspapers, of boxing greats, handsome actors, and the like. One look at Barr and you saw why he favored the arch-typical example of masculinity. I wasn't one, either, but I think I had Barr beat.

Barr was small and thin. He looked like he might break if a hurricane blew through town. Check that. A decent gale might do the trick. He styled his hair in the latest fashion made famous by Hollywood's leading men, but the puffy top of his head wafted in the breeze of the nearby fan.

He stood when Gardner and I approached. My friend made introductions. I gripped Barr's little hand. "Wade here is a bona fide PI."

Barr's eyes widened in awe. Still gripping my hand, he squeezed harder. It could have been your elderly aunt grasp. I had to restrain myself.

"Pleased to meet you, Mr. Barr." I gave my hand a gentle tug. "Mind if I have that back?"

"Oh, right, right, right," Barr muttered, suddenly

noticing his own cluttered desk. "I'm not usually this messy."

"Don't care." I placed a hand on his shoulder. I swear I felt his collar bone through his suit. "I need to ask you about the police beat from last week."

He stood straighter, as if President Roosevelt himself had just asked a favor. "What do you need to know?"

Gardner hooked a thumb at Barr. "He hears a lot of things over the police band and forgets little."

"Good. Last week, there was a ruckus out west of town. Some sort of police chase and a fugitive running through some farm land and such."

Barr snapped his fingers. "I know what you're talking about. It was a burglary in progress. Three units were called out. One was close to the house in question and got there before the others did. Two officers went up to the house and knocked. The burglar, hearing the cops show up, took off out back. They gave chase, but lost him."

Gardner gave me an admiring look. "See what I mean?"

I nodded. "Excellent. What day did you publish that? I need it for the time line I'm making."

"Oh, it was last Tuesday, but we didn't publish it."

"Didn't publish it? But you seem to know all the details."

"It was on the police band, and I've got a friend down at the station, but it was one of the cases we didn't publish."

Gardner asked, "Why not? Space considerations?"

Barr thought for a moment. "No, not really. The boss reviews the stuff I write and makes decisions. Sometimes it's for space, other times it's just something the police don't want published. It happens sometimes."

"Which was it this time?"

Barr pursed his lips. "Don't know."

I stepped forward and sat on the edge of his desk. "Just now, you gave a detailed rundown of what happened that night. From the way you described it, the chase was just a chase. But why was the man running?"

"I'm not sure. The location seemed a bit out of the way, you know. It was west of here, out past downtown, out toward the country. It was that part of town where the farms come right up against the new ritzy neighborhood. I forgot the name of the area, Tanglewood maybe?"

I thought about that area of town. It was relatively new, full of nice homes and well-manicured lawns. However, the poorer farmland jutted right up against it. I suspected, given a decade or two, the farms would be gone and new houses would occupy that land. "Did you happen to hear the address the cops gave each other? You know, where the other units had to get to?"

Barr opened a drawer and pulled out a thick hardbound notebook. It looked more like a bank ledger than a journal, but he opened it and thumbed a few pages back from the end. Running a finger down the page, he stopped. "Here you go. It was 1888 Meadowlark Lane."

I pulled my own notebook and flipped a few pages until I found the address of my client. 1868 Blackbird Lane. Whoever built that land must have loved birds. "You got a city map?"

We all went to one of the center walls of the news room and stood in front of a large map that showed the major and minor roads of Houston, including the train tracks and the path of Buffalo Bayou. I picked up the county atlas and found the grid where Meadowlark Lane was located. It was a north-south street in the northwest part of the county, outside the city limits. Sure enough, parallel to Meadowlark, was Blackbird.

I turned and looked at the two of them. "Who lives at 1888 Meadowlark Lane?"

"As background to my story, I had to find out. Oliver Aldridge lives there with his wife and two kids. He's a banker at University Savings and Loan over near Rice Institute."

Gardner must have seen the blood drain from my face. "What's wrong, Wade?"

My mouth decided to imitate a drought and the pit of my stomach went on a vacation to my shoes. My voice suddenly sounded like a frog. "I know Aldridge. We have," I said, pausing for the right word, "history."

Gardner eyed me closely. "What kind of history?"

"From back on the force. But that doesn't have any play here." I felt like changing the subject fast. "So, the police are called out to Aldridge's house on account of a burglary. They show up, but the thief hightails it out of there. Somewhere along the way, the chase makes its way to my client's farm. He hears things, but nothing comes of it. A day or so later, he gets the order from the county that his birds have to be killed." I tapped my finger on the map. "Why?"

Gardner said, "If the burglary was at the Aldridge place, was there a police report filed?"

"Don't know," Barr said. "Once the boss told me not to run the story, I stopped doing research."

I gave Gardner a funny look. "Care for a ride to the station? Maybe we can find a copy of the police report."

Gardner looked around the news room. Most of the reporters had their heads down, plying their trade. Across the room, Johnny Flynn sat at Gardner's old desk, pounding away at his typewriter. Gardner sighed. "Ever since I got demoted, I ain't even had a sniff at a juicy story. My editor has kept me far away from any investigative reporting. In fact, the owner might even fire me if I write one."

"So, that's a no?"

"Are you kidding? Let me get my hat."

CHAPTER SEVEN

The Houston Police station was on Caroline Street just south of the main downtown area. It was built in 1923 and looked it. Low, squat, and without much room to operate on the inside, it was not for nothing that a fair number of cops preferred the heat on the street to the stifling heat inside. Getting assigned a desk job should have been covered with hazard pay.

Gardner and I strolled into the sauna and right up to the desk sergeant. It was a pleasure to take out hats off. The name on the man's tag read Jones. He wasn't one I knew. I deferred to Gardner to see if his magical reporter skills could gain us entrance.

"Gordon Gardner of the Post-Dispatch. We're here to ask some questions about a burglary last week."

Jones gave Gardner a skeptical eye. "Gardner? Ain't you supposed to be hobnobbing with the fancy folks? I got tole I ain't gotta talk to you. Besides, yer sniffin' up the wrong tree. Ain't nothin' here you need."

"It's part of a society story. Involves Oliver Aldridge. All we want is to talk with someone who was at the scene last week. This was out west off 18th Street, northwest side, Meadowlark Lane."

"Who's this guy?" Jones turned his attention to me.

"I'm nobody," I said, trying to keep the conversation going. "You don't even see me."

Jones, who wore horn-rimmed glasses, peered at me. "I see you, mister. You standing right there."

Subtlety. The thing you can't teach a good cop. "I'm just here for moral support. My friend here is going to write a story about the burglary last week and how numerous units were called out to chase the suspect." I turned to Gardner. "If our sources are correct, I believe the suspect got away. Am I right?"

"Right as rain," Gardner chimed in.

"Aren't you looking to write a piece that is as fair and balanced as possible?" I looked directly at Gardner.

He held up his hands in a mock scale of justice. "The only way."

I turned back to Jones. "But if we don't have solid facts to ground the piece, I'm not sure if my friend here, honest a reporter as he is, can write a balanced piece. You see what I mean?"

Jones eyed me with a mixture of contempt and befuddlement. I pressed in on him. "All we need is the name of an officer at the scene. Or of the lead detective."

Jones smiled, like he just got a joke told to him an hour ago. "I know just the person that can handle your request." He stood. "Follow me."

Gardner and I exchanged glances. He shrugged, I

shrugged, but we carried our hats in our hands as we followed Jones from the main foyer into the heated heart of the police station.

Various detectives, officers, and beat cops looked up as we strolled through the open room. I got a few looks of recognition, a couple of mouth-breathers with hung jaws, and a few fingers pointed my way.

"I see you're still loved around here," Gardner said.

"They send me flowers every week."

We rounded a familiar corner of the office and beelined it towards an office. I stopped dead in my tracks.

"What's up?" Gardner said.

"It's Burman." I closed my eyes and shook my head. "He's taking us to see Burman."

Another voice spoke from behind me. "If you want to see me, Wade, all you gotta do is turn around."

Gardner looked over my shoulder to see Police Captain Oscar Burman come up beside me and plant a burly arm around my shoulders. "Hello, Wade. What brings your carcass back to the station?"

I bit the inside of my lip to keep my mouth shut. There were any of a dozen words that I wanted to say in regard to Captain Burman, none of them polite. Burman wasn't necessarily a bad guy, but if you got on his bad side, you'd better watch out because, sooner or later, he'd get you.

Back in my beat cop days, Burman got assigned to investigate me when the unpleasantness arose. He did his job, but he didn't listen to any of my explanations, truthful as they were about the bigger picture. Burman only saw what he wanted to see: a cop whose behavior tainted the department. The only thing that would fix that would be to kick me off the force.

He did. Now I'm a shamus, trying to make my way in the world without a badge.

Gardner, of course, knew the entire story, and persuaded his editors to let him write the story even though everyone knew we were pals. He pulled a few punches, including the big one, but not many. Like he told me, wouldn't you want an old friend to write the story that's going to be written anyway? Sound familiar?

"Captain," Gardner said, "how are you today?"

"I was better until I saw this guy." He gave my shoulders a sharp tug then released me. "Don't let his reputation taint your writing, Gardner."

Again, the words bubbled up from inside me, but Gardner spoke before any of them could be uttered. "Captain, let's not forget that Mr. Wade here helped foil that Nazi plot. I believe even the Army intelligence officers publicly thanked him. Cut him some slack."

"I did. Back when he was a cop. He made himself a noose."

I scowled at that, but set aside my rebuttal. "We're

looking into a burglary that happened last week."

The captain shook out a cigarette from his rumpled pack and lit it. "We have lots of burglaries. Which one in particular?"

"Out on Meadowlark Lane."

Burman cocked an eyebrow. Giving Jones his chin, Burman dismissed the young man. Jones quietly scooted away. "Look, I won't even dignify your request with a trip to my office. There's no crime out there. No police report filed. Nothing."

"Really?" I gave Gardner a quick look, then glanced back to Burman. "We heard differently. We heard there was a whole police chase, two, three units all converging on the fancy house out there."

Burman puffed his cheeks and shook his head. "Well, there might've been something you might've heard on the police band but it was ultimately nothing." He hooked a thumb at Gardner. "I think your source was mistaken."

I'd seen more obvious hints in poker games. Clearly, this wasn't the route to take. "C'mon, Gardner, it's getting a little hot in here. I need some fresh air."

Gardner didn't want to leave. He was ready to keep at Burman until he gave up the name, but a slight tilt of my head toward the exit delayed that outburst. He nodded and followed me out. The eyes of the other officers and detectives all bore into me.

Once outside, Gardner said, "Why'd we just leave? There's more to the story than he's letting on. My reporter's sense can feel that."

"My detective sense feels it, too, but we ain't gonna get anywhere with Burman. If the chief is the one that got your editor to kill the story, then Burman's just the wall. We need to go around the wall."

"The source?"

I smiled. "I told you I wanted some fresh air."

CHAPTER EIGHT

The West 18th Street extension was an east-west street just northwest of downtown. On the east side, it ended in the Heights, a little suburb of Houston noted for—what else—its higher elevation. That wasn't a stretch since Houston itself is pretty flat. On the west side, it ended at State Highway 6, the only way to get to Austin. In between, you had a funny mixture of farms and fancy houses of rich folks who liked the luxury of country life with the convenience of the nearby city.

It was off West 18th that both my client and Oliver Aldridge lived. Sitting in my car, Gardner and I looked at the close proximity of the two pieces of land. The Aldridge mansion was the last in a string of high-class homes with wide yards and trees. After it, poorer farm land started.

Gardner said, "It's only a matter of time before the rich just take over that land. Maybe this is the first salvo."

"Maybe." I pointed across one of the fields. "That's Smith's house. Looks like he grows corn and raises chickens." I pointed to the last house of a rich man. "And that's Aldridge's house. If a thief ran out the back, I can see where Smith's farm would be the easy escape route."

Gardner looked down at the map of the city and traced his finger along one of the lines. "According to this map, there's another farm road back there. And there's one on the west side of the Smith farm." He looked up and back through the windshield. "If the cops never caught the thief but chased him all the way to Smith's farm, I'm betting he stashed his car on that road and made a clean getaway."

"Or that's where the thief's partner was." I started the car.

"Where we going?"

I nodded to the Aldridge house. "Front door. Let's be upfront and see what happens."

To call this house was a mansion was doing the word a disservice. There was a nice line of larger-than-necessary homes on this stretch of road, but the Aldridge home had all the other ones beat. If my estimate was correct, the Aldridge property was, in fact, two lots joined into one. The circular drive was ready for a limo to cruise in there and not need any room to back up. The house itself was a three-story job, complete with a second-floor balcony. The entire structure was done up in a style of a Spanish villa, with ceramic tiles on the roof and stucco along the walls. That's definitely one way to beat the Texas heat.

I rapped my knuckles on the door, then grasped the brass door knocker and repeated the entreaty. Footsteps were heard from inside the house. The door opened. Sure enough, a butler gazed out into the afternoon sun.

"May I help you?" His words and voice oozed out

like smooth gin in a martini.

"Yes. My name is Wade. I'm a private investigator. I'm looking into the burglary that happened here last week, and I'd like to talk with the lady"—I checked my watch—"or the gentleman of the house, if they're available."

His eyes were perpetually half-lidded. "I'm sorry, sir, but they are both gone. Mr. Aldridge is at the office and Mrs. Aldridge is out."

"She drive herself?"

"Beg pardon?"

"Does she drive her own car or is there a chauffeur?"

"I'm afraid I'm not at liberty to discuss Mrs. Aldridge's driving habits."

"Great, I'll take that to mean she prefers to drive herself because she likes the freedom but her husband insists on a driver to make sure she's safe. And, since the driver's here, that means she's probably inside, wishing she could just get in her car and drive away."

The half-lidded eyes widened a bit.

I pushed ahead. "So, do we get to see Mrs. Aldridge or do we start hollering?" I jerked a thumb over my shoulder. "You suppose the neighbors will mind if I honked my horn?"

The distaste in the butler's face was pronounced.

"Sir, I'm not in the habit of being bullied at my place of employment."

"That's okay. I'm used to being ignored. But this guy's not." I indicated Gardner. "Know who he is? He's a reporter with the Post. He's writing a piece on the burglary. I know he'd really like to have actual facts for his story. We both know the Post runs quality journalism, but, well, you know. He also writes fiction. The pulps. You read those?"

"I do not, sir." The butler's temper was starting to sizzle.

"So, since you're being an obstacle, we'll just be on our way. C'mon, Gordon." I said it louder than the butler wanted. I was rewarded with a grimace.

We moved backward toward my car when a female voice spoke from above us. "It's okay, Randolph. I'll see them."

Gardner craned his neck to see who had spoken.

I just smiled.

Randolph, keeping his seething to a bare minimum, showed both Gardner and me into the upstairs solarium. It had windows on two sides. The sun steamed in and glistened off the ceramic tiles on the floor. In the middle of the room was an easel with a canvas. A still life, fruits in a bowl. Looked like Mrs. Aldridge fancied herself a painter. I could tell what I was looking at, but she was a far cry from good.

The woman herself was a specimen. Blond, thin, with curves that could send a man into vertigo just looking at them, Sarah Aldridge stood with the confident self-assurance of one who knew her place in society, knew that she looked good and had men ogling her all the time, and knew what she wanted and likely to get it. She stood in front of the easel, a painter's palette hooked around one thumb and a brush in the other. She didn't turn when we came into the room.

"Thank you, Randolph." she dismissed him with her tone. The butler gave us a last stink eye and glided out of the room.

"I supposed you both want to know what happened last week." Single-malt scotch was not as smooth as that voice. "Isn't that why you threatened my butler?"

I stepped forward, angling to get a look at her face. She had yet to turn, but the hair was swept up in a gentle twist on her head, a few loose strands hanging down to her neck. I wanted to see if her face matched the figure. "My name's Wade. I'm a private investigator. This is Gordon Gardner from the Post. Yes, we're following up on the burglary last week."

Still without turning, she said, "I understand why Mr. Gardner's here, assuming he's telling the truth." She put the finishing touches on one of the oranges and placed the brush onto the table next to the easel. "What I want to know is why you're here."

She turned. Light from one of the windows caught her hair and made it glow. Stunning was too mild a word; it didn't do Sarah Aldridge justice. The high cheek bones, the full lips, the gossamer skin were traits any woman would kill to have. She had them all, but she also had the coup de grace: her eyes. The light green eyes of the Caribbean Sea. You could get lost in them. I did right then.

Gardner caught me napping. "Sometimes Mr. Wade here likes to think before he speaks." He nudged me.

Sarah smiled. "That's a good habit to have. More men should have it."

I cleared my throat. "I'm investigating the burglary last week."

"Did my husband hire you?"

"No."

"Then I don't see why you're here. If we didn't hire you and we didn't file a police report, how are you even on a case?"

The verbal slap was enough to jolt me back to my accustomed self. "I've been hired by one of your neighbors to look into the disturbance."

She frowned, but still looked beautiful. "What business is it of theirs what goes on down here? We practically own the street."

I held my tongue, letting her stew a moment longer. "Were you here last week when the burglar broke in?"

"I'm afraid I can't answer that." She was playing with me now. "I still don't know why you landed on my doorstep."

I inhaled deeply and decided to be honest. "I've been hired by one of your neighbors on the other side to look into the events of last week."

She screwed up her face in disgust. "One of them?" She seemed genuinely appalled. "How in the world can they afford it?"

I shrugged. "Be that as it may, my client raises chickens. A few days after the police chased your burglary suspect through his farm and chicken barnyard, he got an order that all his chickens have to be slaughtered. Now, we know there was a large police presence here last week. It was on the police band. It was going to be public knowledge in the newspaper before someone pulled rank and killed the story. Sure, it was just a police beat little write-up, but, still, it would have been in print. And now it's not. So, tell me, Mrs. Aldridge, what was stolen here last week?"

She gazed at me, studying me, for what, I didn't know. Maybe she was trying to figure me out. It's usually not that hard. I'm a pretty straightforward guy. But she stared at me, and then through me, like I wasn't even there.

"What did the police report say?"

Gardner frowned. "What police report?"

Sarah smiled. "Exactly. There is no police report, so there must not have been a crime."

"But there were a half-dozen squad cars out here," I said. "Surely there was something going on."

Her shrug was a minimal gesture, like she didn't even bother mustering up the energy for an honest-to-goodness shrug. "That's all there is to it."

"That's your story, then?" I said.

"It is."

"Then, if you don't mind, why don't you tell me what you heard or saw last week?"

She fingered one of her brushes. I watched her hands. They were model's hands, the kind you'd see in a magazine ad. There were paint splotches on them but not many. It was like the paint decided it wasn't worth the effort to blemish such unblemishable hands.

"What night was it?" she asked.

"Last Tuesday."

"Oh, I was out that night. Oliver took me to dinner and then out dancing. It was quite a nice time. One of the big touring bands was in town. They were magnificent. Count Basie, I think."

"So, you're saying you weren't even here when the police showed up?"

"Right. My husband and I were out on the town.

"Then who called the police?"

She paused a moment that barely registered. "Perhaps one of the neighbors?"

"What about Randolph? He looks like he's smart enough to use a phone."

The fire in her eyes all but scorched me. "You will leave my butler or anyone else in my employ out of your so-called investigation. If you have any questions, you will only speak to me or my husband."

Gardner said, "Your neighbors. Y'all ever get together and gossip, talk about the other neighbors?"

She cooled a bit and gave Gardner her eyes. "I play bridge with three of the women on the street, but we had to postpone our game last Thursday on account of sickness. One of the ladies caught a cold."

Convenient, I thought.

Gardner said, "When y'all got back from your night on the town, did you happen to notice all the police cars? Maybe even the flashing lights?"

"There were no police cars in the area when we got home. It was just as dark as it always is."

"Your husband. He at work?"

"He is, and I bet he wouldn't be too happy with your line of questioning."

"Probably not," I agreed, "but we have to ask."

"True, but I don't have to answer. And I'd like to have you both leave now."

"But we're not finished," Gardner said. "There's still too much left to ask."

I grabbed his shoulders and turned him toward the door. There was clearly nothing more to learn from her. She was either covering for someone or, in the more unlikely case, she truly didn't know.

CHAPTER NINE

We took most of the rest of the day to talk with all the rich folks on the one side of the West 18th Street extension. As expected, not all of Aldridge's neighbors were home the night of the burglary. Those who remembered it got vague when pressed for details. The long and short of it was that we got nothing consequential in the way of leads.

The only thing close to forward movement in this case came when Gardner and I paid a visit to the farmers on the other side of the Smith farm. Over glasses of just about the best lemonade I had ever tasted, Otis and Aileen Johnson told us about the police chasing some dark figure near their land. When Otis went to fetch his shotgun, the family heard the footsteps cross their land and out to FM 476. A few seconds later, the sound of a car engine filled the silence and the car raced away.

Satisfied with the confirmation that someone was definitely fleeing the police but coming up short on every other front, Gardner and I drove back to town. We talked about the war in Europe, the likelihood that the U.S. would get in it, and the other news, much of which pretty much dealt with the war. When sovereign nations are fighting each other and their colonies around the world are being threatened and taking up arms, that kind of thing tends to dominate all discussion.

I dropped Gardner off in front of the news building and sat in the car a few moments. I wasn't getting anywhere with the Smith case and the clock was ticking. Something had to break, and fast.

Remembering the punch I had taken from Peete that day at lunch, I touched my sore jaw. The two things had to have a connection, right? Clara's suddenly getting a new man in her life and this chicken-slaughter order.

Throwing the car in gear, I circled the block for an open meter. I fed a dime into the machine and walked half a block to a pay phone. After a nickel found a new home, the HPD dispatcher answered the call.

"Leroy Dwight, please."

The dispatcher relayed the call. A few moments later, my old police pal answered the phone.

"Leroy, it's Wade."

"Wade, you old son of a gun. What the hell you doing calling me? I heard about your little visit today."

"Yeah. Well, I needed to verify something and Burman did exactly that. You still staying out of trouble?"

"Sure am, a fact you'd know if you actually gave a damn during times when you didn't want something. That's why you're calling, isn't it? You want something."

The bitterness in his voice was palpable. During the

times when the internal investigation was ongoing and my time as a Houston police officer was coming to an end, Leroy Dwight was one of the few friends who stuck with me. He deflected all the crap that got thrown his way, letting it roll off his shoulders. He defended me to anyone who'd listen. It didn't matter that I had to resign, he still believed in me.

And I continually abused that relationship from time to time. He was still on the force, moving up to the detective ranks. He was good, too. Bulldog-like. But we found ourselves on opposite sides of the equation more often than not. The only thing that helped was when I got him out of a jam. With me being a PI, I was able to do things and go places he couldn't. I helped him and he felt he owed me. I didn't disabuse him of that notion, but I got to thinking that my welcome was wearing thin.

"Look, Leroy, I know you stuck with me back then, but I figured you'd best be served by not being seen with me."

"I can do my own living, Wade. That includes the people with whom I choose to spend time." He was always a proper grammar kind of guy. "I wish you'd come around more often. Rosemary does, too."

His wife was a dandy gal. We both saw her at a dance one night. Their eyes locked on each other and I just vanished from the scene.

"I'll make a note to come by and play gin rummy and

drink cocktails."

"Right. When you're darkening my door, I'll believe it. What do you want?"

"I'm on a case right now…"

"Same one?"

"Well, that's the thing. I'm not sure, but I think two cases might have a link. You ever heard of a man named Amos Peete?"

The short bark of a laugh came through loud and clear through the phone. "Of course I know him. I've even busted him."

My pulse quickened. "What can you tell me about him?"

There was some silence on Leroy's end of the line. "I'm not sure I should talk here about him."

"Why?"

"Someone might hear."

I frowned, then remembered he couldn't see me. "Why would somebody care if you were talking about Peete?"

"Because of who he is and what he's done."

"Leroy, spill at least something to me. What's he done?"

"He's a killer, Wade. A hired killer."

The bottom of my stomach just went a little deeper. I started to wonder if Clara had the name correct. Maybe it was another guy name Amos Peete. Unlikely, I thought. Not with the kind of behavior he showed that morning. "Talk to me, Leroy. Give me some details."

More silence from his end. "Listen, I'm off in a half hour. Meet me outside Foley's. We'll talk face to face."

"Why all the hush-hush?"

"Just meet me, okay?" He hung up.

Curiosity got the better of me. That, and something else. A protective quality seeped through me.

On a whim, I threw another nickel into the phone and dialed the health department. A woman answered. "May I speak to Clara Milbanks, please?"

There was an awkward pause. The woman didn't know what to do with a caller who wanted to speak to a receptionist. "One moment, please."

I lit a cigarette waiting for Clara to come on the line. When she did, I told her who I was. "Listen, do you have a friend you can stay with?"

"I have a few, but none I'm close enough to ask that kind of question. Why?"

I hesitated, then spoke a version of the truth. "I just want to make sure you're safe. What's your home telephone number?"

"You trying to pick me up, Mr. Wade?"

"No, I'm trying to protect you while I look into this deeper. Am I the only one you've told?"

"Yes."

"That's why I need your home number, in case I need to contact you."

"Mohawk 4-7217."

"And your address."

A slight pause. "3921 Spruce Street. Say, what's all this about?"

"Not entirely sure, but I'm about to meet a guy with some more answers. I'll talk to you later. But listen, watch your back. I'll see if I can stop by later on."

I could hear the smile in her tone. "Mr. Wade, I do think you're trying to pick me up."

"Suit yourself." I hung up.

I hopped back into my car and drove to Foley's. Finding yet another meter, I got out and leaned against a light pole. I only had to wait for two cigarettes.

A little after five, Leroy Dwight, dressed in his plain clothes that just screamed cop, sauntered up to me.

"Thanks for meeting me," I said.

"No problem. Just wanna give you the whole story. Bum a cigarette?"

I gave him one and lit it. He exhaled his first puff. "Tell me how you've come to know Peete."

I told him about my two cases and how one of the persons of interest had had some contact with Peete. I even gave him the rundown on my own contact with the killer. I had the bruised jaw to prove it.

"You're lucky he only punched you in the jaw. He's gutted other folks."

"How do you know this?"

"Rumor, mostly. The criminals in this town are a tight bunch. They tend to keep to themselves, even if they're in rival groups. Word spreads when a man of Peete's talent shows up in the dugout."

"What's his specialty?"

"He's a knife man."

I shook my head. I'd almost prefer a gun man. Then I'd be on the same level. A knife man preferred everything close and personal. That didn't bode well for Clara Milbanks. Or for me.

Leroy gave me a serious look. "Wade, as your friend, I have to tell you to watch yourself. If Peete has it out for someone, chances are he'll get'em. You get in the way, well…." He shrugged.

CHAPTER TEN

Later that evening, I took Leroy up on his gin rummy offer. I showed up at his house, bottle of wine in hand. Rosemary had made a nice, home-cooked meal of roast beef and carrots. I don't mind cooking and do more than I eat out, but there's something about a woman's touch in the kitchen that a bachelor like me just doesn't have.

The evening was fine, and I even enjoyed Leroy's two kids, Leroy III and Rebecca. I went home and spent lots of waking time staring at the ceiling as lit by the streetlamp knifing through my Venetian blind.

The next morning, after a breakfast of ham and eggs and coffee, I found myself back in my office interviewing possible secretaries. I was itching to get back out on the pavement and do something, but a couple of things stopped me. The first was Stella, my sister. She had agreed to spearhead the search for a new secretary by lining up a few women for me to interview. Not sure where she got them, but most of them were not what I was looking for. Sure, they typed well enough, but all were slower than Martha from the day before.

The more pressing matter was I didn't know what to do next. I basically kept staring through the women I was supposedly interviewing until I heard a commotion in the main office. The blonde sitting opposite me, the last one on the list I had, turned around as the door to my inner office opened. Martha Weber stood there, hips cocked. She held up her hand and rubbed her thumb and forefinger together.

"I left yesterday, Wade, and you didn't pay me the balance you owe me." Her eyes flicked to the blonde, then back to me. "Five dollars?"

The blonde turned back and gave me a what-the-hell look. I smiled and held up my hand, hoping to stave off any comment. "Just a minute." I reached around to my wallet.

The blonde asked, "You already hired a secretary? Why am I even here?"

"No, I haven't hired anyone yet," I mumbled, unfolding my wallet and stealing a glance inside. With the advance Smith had given me yesterday, the cash I had on hand was substantially greater than it had been yesterday. I partially hid the wallet behind my desk since I didn't want Martha or the blonde—what was her name?—to see the extra cash.

Pulling out a fiver, I stood and held it out between two fingers. Martha walked over and took it from me. She gave me a little smile and something akin to a wink.

"Thanks for helping out yesterday."

"You're welcome," Martha said. "Any closer to making a hire?"

I scowled. "Not really."

She looked mildly hurt. The blonde batted her eyelashes, trying to improve her chances. "Well, then, I hope you come to a decision soon. I have other offers, you know, but your job looks like more fun."

Looking at her face, something tugged at me, but I couldn't put it in place. I was a little peeved that she had burst into my office like that, but then a thought occurred to me. A big goofy grin spread across my face.

"Thanks," I said.

"For what?" Martha asked.

"For reminding me what a PI can do."

Thirty minutes later, I sat in my car, newspaper in hand, and fortified with a fresh pack of cigarettes and a cup of coffee. I had parked half a block down from the agriculture office. Martha's barging into my office bullying me for her payment had given me an idea: I could strong-arm Teague into rescinding the slaughter order.

By the time lunch rolled around, I had read through the entire paper, done the crossword, and emptied the coffee. Teague strolled outside, putting his hat on his head. He looked one way and then the other. Plunging his hands into his pockets, he walked at a brisk pace in my direction. I waited until he passed my car before I opened the door and got out.

It was lunchtime and the streets were crowded. I was trying to figure out how best to corner him and give him some powerful reasons why he needed to cancel the slaughter. I was going to need to get him in an alley so we could talk in "private."

Sauntering up behind him, I sized up my opportunities. A block and a half away, I saw the perfect place: an alley between tall buildings that would provide enough cover from any looky-loos and long enough to dampen any yell Teague was bound to emit.

I matched his stride on his blind right side. When we had cleared the corner of the alley, I reached over, grabbed his upper arm in my grip and, as nonchalantly as possible, shoved him into the alley.

"Hey." He turned to see who was moving him.

"Quiet."

He must have recognized my voice. "You're that PI dick, aren't you?"

"Forgot my name already?" I led him deeper into the alley.

Teague slowed his pace and pushed back.

"Look," I said, "I just want to talk."

"No you don't. You're planning to harass me, knock me around, aren't you?"

I wasn't used to having folks guess my moves,

especially not pencil-pushers like Teague. With a quick little gesture, he cleared my grip and turned to face me.

"If you're trying to strong arm me, Mr. Wade," he said, standing straighter and turning to face me, "it won't work."

Involuntarily, I balled my hands into fists. "Why not?"

"Because you have nothing with which to change my mind."

I showed him one of my mitts. "Wanna bet?"

"It won't change anything, I assure you." He shrank a little at my bluster but still retained an air of calm. "You see, there are powerful forces that have already pointed me in the direction I have to take." He paused and adjusted his tie.

"Who's doing this? Who's telling you to kill those chickens?"

A shadow crossed over his countenance and his visibly shuddered. He was answering my questions internally. "It's not a "who." It's a "they." And when they speak, you listen and act."

Frowning, I said, "What kind of a group is that powerful? The government? Aldridge's cronies?"

"When you deal with this group, it makes those you named seem like amateurs." He righted his hat and folded his arms. "You can beat me and punch me or do whatever to me because I'm not afraid of you. I am afraid of them and I'm going to damn well do what they say. Yes, they're paying me, but that's just business." He paused, giving me a funny look. "So, are you going to do me harm? Or are you too chicken to try anything?"

I wanted to, very much. But now my curiosity was aroused. "What is this group?"

"I am not at liberty to divulge that information. Suffice it to say their influence is greater than that of any other organization I've ever known. I respect them, but I fear them more. And that's why I'll do exactly what they say."

"And that's to kill my client's chickens?"

He nodded.

Stupidly, I realized my fists were still hanging in the air. I lowered them, defeated.

Teague nodded once. "Good day, Mr. Wade."

CHAPTER ELEVEN

I spent the lunch hour downing iced tea and a hot dog from a street vendor. I tried to reconstruct my confidence after Teague's seemingly fearless face in front of my fists. The longer I sat, the more I realized there was still one other option to follow: Danielle Bowie.

Killing the afternoon in my office by reviewing all the resumes for the women who wanted to be my secretary, I drove back to the health inspector's office a half hour before closing time.

The more I thought about it, the more something nagged at me. I couldn't help wondering about Danielle and the stranger who had come to Teague's office to threaten Teague. He had thought Clara was Danielle. Why? And why did that make a difference?

Positioned across the street behind a tall tree, I stood and smoked and waited for five o'clock. When it rolled over, I stubbed out the butt and kept my eyes peeled not only for Danielle Bowie but Amos Peete as well.

Clara emerged first. She took a right and walked down the street. She hopped a bus and was gone. Thankfully, I didn't see anyone following her. I'd certainly check up on her later.

Danielle emerged about five minutes later. She walked

the opposite direction and stood at a bus stop with some other patrons. I debated whether to try my luck at getting on the same bus, but decided for the more subtle tactic of following in my car.

Ten minutes later, the bus arrived and Danielle got on. In the bus's exhaust, I trotted across the street and got into my car. I pulled into evening traffic and kept the bus in sight. It wasn't too difficult.

The bus's route took it south and into the West University area. Named pretty obviously for the region just to the west of Rice Institute, West University had a distinct collegiate feel in the middle of the big city. Danielle emerged from the bus and walked up Rice Boulevard. I parked along Kirby and got out. Keeping a discreet distance, I followed her.

She seemed to know exactly where she was going. She moved with a purposeful stride, almost as if she were hurrying. I had to keep moving in order to maintain line of sight.

Arriving at an outdoor restaurant, Danielle talked with the head waiter who then showed her a seat. Less than five minutes later, a man in a nicely pressed suit and tie arrived, fedora cantered at a rakish angle. I thought nothing of him until he sat at the same table as Danielle.

Now I was in a quandary. She had seen me once before and I figured she could make me without any problem. And it was entirely possible he was just a suitor, but I didn't want to take the chance. Something on the man's face teased a memory. Clara had said the man who visited Teague the other night wore a thin mustache, and damn if this guy didn't have a nice, pencil-thin mustache.

This had to be the guy who threatened Teague.

They were going to eat so I figured I might as well, too. I slipped into a deli and bought a corned beef sandwich and a Dr. Pepper. I stood just inside the deli's window eying Danielle and her mystery man. They sat, ate, and talked. I stood, ate, and stayed quiet. When both of them put their napkins on the table, the man pulled a white piece of paper or envelope out of his coat pocket. Laying it flat on the table, he slid it over to her. She deftly put it in her purse and the man called for the check.

I threw away my trash and walked outside. I positioned myself behind a parked car and waited for the pair to leave.

"There's a law against loitering," a voice said from behind me.

I turned and saw the man from the deli standing just inside his door. His apron was mottled with the stains of handling food and having it all splash on him throughout the day. You could almost make out what sandwiches he had made just by looking at that culinary kaleidoscope.

"I'm not loitering." I gave him a warm smile. "I'm just letting the food digest." "No, you're loitering. I have a mind to call the cops."

I smirked at that. Depending on who he might call, I could get lucky and score a beat cop I knew. On the other hand, I might get one of Burman's goons.

I pulled out my wallet. I started to pull out a few bills.

"Look, I don't take no bribes," the man said. "I just follow the law."

Giving him a conspiratorial smile, I said, "Why don't we just keep this little transaction between you and me? We don't have to tell the boss, huh? What do you say?"

"I am the boss," he said with a certain amount of indignation. "But I'm not above taking your cash. And I'm savvy enough to know you ought to get inside or they'll see you."

I whirled around and saw that Danielle and the mystery man had separated. Danielle was walking west, the mystery man hailed a cab. The cabbie dutifully stopped and the mystery man was gone.

Replacing my wallet in my pocket, I moved out to follow Danielle. I didn't give the deli owner a second thought.

Danielle moved with an assurance that all but made me have to trot to keep up. You know how hard it is to do that and still be inconspicuous? Damn near impossible. The patrons walking along the sidewalks would likely remember the strange man moving against the grain of pedestrian traffic with his eyes focused on something across the street.

Danielle moved with speed down the block to the fourth store. She stopped and went in. I angled for a better look and read the name on the sign: Holcombe Jewelry. I pulled out my notebook and jotted down the name. I wasn't familiar with it, but that didn't mean anything. One of the benefits of not having a steady gal on my arm was that it eliminated the need to frequent jewelry stores.

Leaning up next to the wall, I pulled out a cheap pair of binoculars and peered through the window. Danielle was the only patron in the store. The jangling bell had alerted the jeweler and he looked up. A smile creased his face. The smile faltered a bit when she handed him the envelope. The smile died on his face. He went pale when he opened it and read the contents. The jeweler looked up at Danielle and shook his head. She nodded her head. Then she pointed her finger at him and must have said some pretty awful words because he shrank back, then nodded meekly.

Danielle turned. I quickly stowed the field glasses inside my coat and turned to admire women's clothes in the store front. In the reflection, I watched Danielle once more move down the block in her brisk pace. Instead of the bus this time, she hailed a cab. She was gone.

I didn't have long to wait. The jeweler stuck his head out the front door and looked down the street in the direction Danielle had gone. Seeing that she was gone, he turned his sign from "Open" to "Closed" and locked the door. He adjusted his hat lower on his head and made his way to a Chevrolet town sedan parked two slots from the front door. Again, looking both ways, he got into his car and pulled out into the street. Whatever had spooked him was something big. I aimed to find out what it was.

I ran back to my car and climbed behind the wheel. If he got on Kirby, I'd lose him.

Throwing the car into gear, I raced off after him.

CHAPTER TWELVE

Cyrus Holcombe drove purposefully, taking some turns tight and others more leisurely. His commute took us both back to downtown. The sun was setting and, one by one, the lights were coming on. Houston at night is a beautiful sight. There were days when I just looked at the buildings, felt pride in my hometown. I didn't have that luxury tonight. I had a quarry to pursue.

Holcombe drove north through downtown and into the area known as the Heights. Along Heights Boulevard, he finally slowed as he neared a rather large Victorian mansion. I matched his slow-down speed and parallel parked behind a large delivery truck. I slipped out of the car and watched as Holcombe got out of his car, did another spot check of his surroundings, and headed up the stairs to a house. Waiting a few more moments, I sneaked up closer to the house.

Three short raps on the door, followed a few seconds later with four more must have been the passcode. The door opened. In the dim twilight, the yellow porch bulb splashed outside and onto the well-manicured lawn. The man who opened the door was backlit so I didn't get a good look at him.

Giving the open area in the front yard a quick once-over, I tiptoed across it and flattened myself against the side of the house. I looked across the street and prayed no nosy neighbor decided to look outside.

The mansion was two stories tall with a raised porch. The house itself had a crawl space under it to allow the air to cool the building from below. A white picket fence bordered the front yard. Once past the main sidewalk view, the white fence stopped and a standard chain-link fence started. I made my way toward that part of the fence line.

The sun had gone down but the day's heat was only slowly ebbing away. Despite that, two of the windows in the first floor were partial open. From inside what appeared to be some sort of sitting room or parlor, I heard voices. Not surprisingly, I didn't recognize any of them.

I crouched low in the shrubs, making sure I didn't step on any dry twigs. I kept my ears open to listen to sounds from the street but also to what the voices were saying.

"I swear I thought she was working for you," a small frail voice said. It was squeaky, made all the more so by the fear in it. I made a leap and tagged that voice as Holcombe's. "With her previous actions for our group, I assumed she was still with the society. How was I to know she had quit and struck out on her own?"

I pulled out my notebook and pencil. The streetlamps and the yellow glow from inside the mansion gave me more than enough light by which to see. I wrote "society" with a question mark.

"Mr. Holcombe." That voice was deeper than Holcombe's, with a sonorous tone that would have been great on the radio. "No need to panic yet. What did she give you?"

"This," Holcombe said. Despite the crickets, I heard the sound of the envelope opening and a paper unfolding.

"Son of a bitch," Deep Voice said.

Another voice in the room asked, "What is it, Mr. Kruger?"

"Marlowe's asking our jeweler friend here to make him a fake diamond." That was Deep Voice. By association, Deep Voice was Kruger. By the sound of it, he led this little soiree.

Had I heard right? Diamond. In my notebook, I wrote that word, circling the word "diamond" three times just to make sure I knew it was important. As if a diamond were anything other than important.

There was movement in the room and a man suddenly appeared in the window. He was backlit from the lights in the room and the streetlamps didn't cast a strong enough glow for me to get a good look at him.

"All I know is," Kruger said, staring out the window, "Marlowe better damn well not be trying to pass the fake to me." He turned back to face the people in the room. "Any ideas on why he's making such a request?"

"Certainly," said another voice. This guy had a gravelly voice, like sandpaper on rough wood. "He lost it at the farm when he ran from Aldridge's place."

"Why do you think that?" said Kruger.

"Because of the slaughter order," said Gravelly Voice. "And that's the reason that nosy PI is involved."

"Remind me why that's my problem."

More footsteps sounded on the wooden floor. Another figure appeared in the window frame, but this time, the lights helped out. I got a good look at him.

Amos Peete.

My jaw ached in sympathy.

Peete stood at the window, nonchalantly holding a cigarette between his fingers and letting the smoke waft into the air. "The farmer and his lawyer hired the dick to try to find out why the health department has condemned all the chickens for slaughter." Turned out, he was the one with the gravelly voice. "They were the ones who got the injunction against the killings until Monday."

How had they figured that out? Was my agency an open book?

"How's that going?" Kruger said.

"As well as can be expected," Peete said. "The lawyer an't get a new injunction so we just have to wait."

"So why the fake?"

"Marlowe needs to deliver something to you by tomorrow," Peete said. "The injunction put him behind schedule, so now he's desperate. My guess is he was trying to get Holcombe here to make a fake and pass it off to you."

"Dammit," Kruger said.

"And that's not all," Peete continued. "The only true reason he's ordering the slaughter is obvious: he hopes to find the real diamond. Now, what he plans to do with it is anyone's guess, but if he's passed off the fake to you, he might just try and scoot out of town with the real one."

"Peete," Kruger said, "I think you know what needs to be done."

Various images filled my imagination in the pregnant silence that followed. It was in that silence that I heard the soft sound of shoes on grass.

CHAPTER THIRTEEN

I whirled my head around and saw the legs of a man moving slowly to my position from the rear of the house. Had he seen me or was he just making a security sweep? When the legs slowed even more and his pants indicated the man was kneeling down, I knew my answer.

I bolted upright from my hiding place in the bushes and ran. Unfortunately, the direction best for me to escape was away from my car. The pace of the footsteps trailing me told me I'd never have a chance to get in my car and start it even if I were going in that direction. The only thing that mattered now was speed.

Gathering momentum, I put shoe leather on the pavement and sprinted away. I heard the footsteps of the man closing in on me, so near I could hear his breathing. It was getting ragged so I poured on my speed. Grinning, I heard him falling away.

But then I heard the sound of an automobile starting up. Then two. I slowed long enough to give a glance over my shoulder. The man who had given chase stood in the middle of the street, his hands on his knees, breathing hard. From behind him, two cars, their headlights knifing through the night, raced up the street.

That was enough for me.

I immediately cut into the nearest yard, my progress shadowed by tall oak trees. I hoofed it past the house and the car parked in the driveway and vaulted the chain-link fence. Naturally, there was a dog there. His howls pierced the stillness, giving my pursuers a clear idea of my location.

There wasn't anything I could do about the dog, but my hopes of leaving him behind were dashed when other hounds took up the call. It was almost as if they were working against me.

I jumped over another chain-link fence and found myself on the next street over. With the dogs baying, the homeowners now started to stir and look out windows. If I wasn't careful, I'd have a whole street full of witnesses who could nail me with a jury. "Yeah, I saw a strange man, Officer. He ran right through my gardenias."

My only consolation was that the cars still had to go half a block to get to an intersection before they could reach me. Said consolation was dashed when I heard the sounds of men on foot making their way through the yards I had just crossed.

"Damn." I let my mind race for any advantage. The only thing I had was distance and my own unpredictability.

I realized that my flight was now taking me back in the direction of my car, albeit on the parallel street. I had no way of knowing which house on this street corresponded to the house in front of which I had parked my car. I had just settled on picking any house when, through the trees, I saw the rear second story of the house Holcombe had entered. Aha! I wondered if they'd think I'd double back.

Not wanting to take too many chances, I got off the sidewalk and kept running on the grass. The grass dampened my footfalls, but a pursuer with keen ears would hear my steps on the driveways when I passed them.

No matter now. I counted five houses more and turned. It was close enough. Stealthily, I slowed and crept past the windows of the house. Not wanting to alert my pursuers to my climbing the fence, I opened the gate and prayed for a cat. Or, at least, no dog.

Thankfully, there wasn't a dog. There was only a woman enjoying a cigarette. She took one look at me, her eyes bulging from her head. I held a finger to my mouth hoping there might be a shred of discretion in her soul.

Her piercing screech proved me wrong.

The scream was like a carrion call. I knew the men after me would waste no time in zeroing in on me. No more pretense of quiet now. I jumped over the chain-link fence and landed perfectly, still running. I stopped at the edge of the house long enough to gauge where my car was. I had guessed right. It was one address to the east.

Throwing all caution to the wind, I broke away from

the house, exposing myself to the streetlamp's faint glow. Shouts of my pursuers could be heard along with the dogs and the screecher woman. It was a cacophony.

Running full tilt, I plunged my hand into my pocket and found my keys. I held them at the ready and thanked myself that I never locked my door.

Reaching my car, I threw open the door and lunged behind the steering wheel. I banged my foot on the clutch and turned the key.

Now, I pride myself on keeping my car in good working order and the old girl didn't fail me then. She started right up. I threw the car into gear and engineered a U-turn and sped out of the neighborhood as fast as the car could take me. The men in the two chase cars, stuck on the other street, wouldn't be able to overtake me in time.

I cut left, then right, then found my way to Highway 90. I turned into town and put the pedal to the metal. I checked my rearview mirror, but saw no sign of the two cars.

I had made it.

CHAPTER FOURTEEN

With my heart pounding rapidly, I reassessed the situation bringing in the new information I had learned. The thief, this Marlowe person, had stolen a diamond from Aldridge's house and promptly lost it in Smith's chicken farm. The slaughter was ordered, I presumed, so that Marlowe or a crony could investigate each fowl for traces of the diamond. Once he found the real thing, he'd deliver it to Kruger.

Or keep it himself. Why else ask Holcombe to create a fake diamond? Then there was Peete, the knife man. He named the farm as the likely spot where the diamond was. Chances were, he'd go there. I had a strong suspicion he wouldn't care about Mr. or Mrs. Smith's safety. I did, and slowed my car long enough to make another turn. I needed to get out and warn them before Peete found his way there.

Fifteen minutes later, I pulled into the lane leading to Smith's house. The lights were on, the yellow glow slanted into the night. Smith opened the door even before I had reached the front porch. One of his hands was holding something just to the side of the door. I didn't know what it was but assumed it was a rifle. "Who's there?"

"It's me, Mr. Smith." I held up my hands in deference.

"Oh, Mr. Wade, you startled me," he said, his hand now coming into view. He turned on the porch light and stepped out. "What can I do for you tonight?"

I walked forward and stopped at the foot of the steps. "I'd like to go visit your chickens. But first, I need to make a phone call."

Mr. and Mrs. Smith let me into their house and I placed a call to Leroy Dwight.

"Let me guess," Leroy said, "you need something else from me."

"Yes and no."

"Well, what is it?"

I'm not usually one to chat about my cases with members of the police, but I definitely could use a hand. I gave him the short version, emphasizing that the Smith family needed protection but leaving out the fact that a diamond might be lost in the coop.

"So you want a couple of guys to come out there and stand guard?"

"Yup."

"The pay is good?"

"Yup."

"I know a guy I can trust. We'll both be there soon."

A few minutes later, Smith and I both had on work boots—his feet were just one size larger than mine— and work gloves. He and I carried flashlights. Mrs. Smith carried a lantern. Together, the three of us tromped over to the chicken pen and coop.

"A diamond," Mrs. Smith said. "Is that what that man was after?"

"Yes, ma'am. The thief lost the diamond in your chicken coop and, not knowing which chicken might have eaten it, contrived to have all your chickens killed, one by one, and to search for the diamond in the carcasses."

"But he clearly was never a farmer," Smith said. "He never even thought to check the manure. What made you think of it, Mr. Wade?"

"Growing up, my grandfather worked his farm and I'd help him. I always enjoyed getting the eggs but hated when he made me wash the chicken house. I was surprised when I saw all the rocks and pebbles in the crap. My grandfather told me most rocks just pass on through."

"You really think by giving the diamond back to that man he'd let us alone?" Mrs. Smith asked.

"Don't see any reason why he would need to maintain the slaughter." I scowled and stifled a wave of nausea. "What do you do with the manure?"

Smith pointed over to a pile next to the hen house. "We compost it and use it on the garden."

"How often do y'all clean the coop?"

"Every morning," Mrs. Smith said. "Otherwise, it gets to be too much."

I sighed when I examined the mound. It was of moderate size, but still it meant sifting through a pile of manure looking for—well—what amounted to a needle in a haystack. Hey, some clichés just reek with truth. So did manure.

Smith walked over and, with a shovel, divided the manure into three smaller piles. Nodding once, we got to work.

I sat down on an overturned bucket and put my handkerchief around my face. It barely kept the stench away. I had a little system. I'd pick up a small pile and work it through my gloved hands. If I found a chunk of anything, I'd examine it in the light. Every so often, I'd stand and walk over to the hose and wash the junk off the small chunks.

This went on for a few hours. When Leroy and his friend, a man named Morales, arrived, I asked that they station themselves up on the porch. When asked what we were doing, I shook my head and told him we were shoveling shit, just like when I was on the force. The clock wound slowly to midnight. Across the fields and through the corn rows I saw the lights of the rich neighborhood and Aldridge's house. He might be entertaining friends while I had my hand in chicken shit.

A little after eleven, Mrs. Smith cried out. She held

something up to her lantern. Mr. Smith and I gathered around her. In the light, the thing glittered despite the muck caking it. The gem was larger than I expected, large enough to want to kill for.

"I think I found it," she whispered.

"I think you did," I said.

In a reverent voice, she asked, "How much is it worth?"

"Don't know, but if there are men trying to reclaim it and willing to do anything to obtain it, it must be a pretty penny."

I glanced at her. In her eyes, I saw the temptation. She was weighing the price and what that money could do for her and her husband. She was wondering if they could get away with it. There were probably more things running through her mind, but I eased my open hand to her. "Mrs. Smith, please let me have it."

Jealousy flashed across her face. Then a moment of shame. I saw both. She flicked her eyes up at me to see if I had noticed. I gave her a warm understanding face. Mr. Smith didn't see any of it so she wouldn't have to live with his knowledge. She turned her hand over and dropped the gem into my palm.

"Thank you."

We stood and looked at the diamond.

Mr. Smith said, "That should do it, right?"

"Pretty sure."

"What are you going to do with it?"

"Turn it over to its rightful owner."

CHAPTER FIFTEEN

Determining the rightful owner proved more of a challenge than I had gambled on. Driving home, I tossed up the various possibilities in my head. I could easily give this diamond to Kruger, the man who wanted it in the first place and hired Marlowe to steal it. It was the loss of the diamond that prompted the order to slaughter Smith's chickens, which was, after all, the sole reason I had been hired.

On the other hand, the diamond seemed to belong to Oliver Aldridge. It was from his safe that it had been stolen. Wasn't he the rightful owner, no matter how irritated that made Kruger? If I turned it over to Aldridge, shouldn't that eliminate all the unpleasantness?

I pondered the question all the way home and into my house. Closing the door behind be, a bone-deep weariness descended on me. I was just about to fall asleep standing up, but I moseyed to the kitchen for a quick nip of whiskey. I smelled my clothes and realized I needed a shower before ruining my sheet. Whiskey first. Shower second. I peeled off my suit and sniffed it. Sure, it reeked, but I seemed to have avoided staining it with chicken shit.

I washed my hands three times, just to be sure all the manure was gone. Getting the ice and clinking the cubes in my glass, I swore I'd never tasted whiskey that good and that cold. I hid the diamond in what I hoped was a good spot. I knew I needed a shower, but I just wanted to sit for a minute. Just a minute. I fell onto the couch. I didn't even take the time to remove my shoes.

I didn't even realize I had fallen asleep until I started awake.

Normally, I am a deep sleeper. Not much wakes me. But that night, something soft did. It was the click of something metallic. In my dream state, I half thought it was my own snores that woke me. I opened and closed my mouth a few times, tasting the dryness in it. It felt like a sandy desert. I was parched. I needed another drink.

I sat up, the springs creaking under my weight. It was then that I realized I was still dressed. I glanced at my watch. Too dark to see. I moved it so that the light from the streetlamp streaming through my blinds caught the hands on my watch. Three in the morning. Sheesh. When was the last time I was awake at that time of night?

I don't know about you, but I can tell when another person is in the same room even if I can't see anyone. As I sat there on my couch, ready to go to the kitchen, I felt the presence of someone. I couldn't explain how, but I did. Trepidation started to warp my mind. It was the middle of the night. Perhaps I was just imagining it. Perhaps there really wasn't anybody in my house.

Then again, I also thought I had closed the Venetian

blind on my east window.

I tensed. The fog of fatigue evaporated. The click I heard must have been the click of the window lock. But if that was the case, then the intruder would have been outside, right? How in the world could the window latch have been opened from the outside?

It was then that I turned my eyes to the door. It was closed. I knew that because there was no light coming from around the frame. Additionally, it was in deep shadow so most things, including my hat rack, were practically in the dark.

But there was a shape standing in front of the door that didn't belong. The shape was a man. I could barely make out the outline, but it was distinctive enough.

Damn. There was someone in my house, and it didn't take three guesses to know why. The diamond.

There were no available weapons near at hand. My gun was in my bedroom. Lot of good it did me there. The question now was: would he let me get to the kitchen and get a knife? Chances were not good in that regard.

The alternative was simple: rush him and get the upper hand. The ache in my head made me wish I hadn't partaken of two shots of rye. I needed more sleep. But I needed to have that intruder out of my house more.

I stood and wobbled a moment. Were I a better actor, I could have thrown in some histrionics, making it appear I was more far gone than I truly was. Maybe throw my arms up.

I think he sensed he was made. I turned to the kitchen. He rushed me. Damn, he was fast. He tackled me full on my right side. This guy, whoever he was, probably had played football on some team. If not, he needed to try out. He'd be a killer linebacker.

As it was, he basically ran over me. The force of his charge clipped my thigh and sent me headlong over the arm of the couch. The side table couldn't take our combined weight and cracked under the strain. The sound of the wood snapping filled the room like a gunshot. The lamp fell to the floor, the bulb smashing to pieces. The lampshade tore off its stand and rolled across the floor.

I grunted. My assailant laughed.

We ended up half on the couch and half on the floor. Our legs were over the armrest while our upper bodies were on the floor. I jammed an elbow behind me but only met with air. The guy rewarded my efforts with a hard finger that jabbed in my exposed armpit.

I swore at the pain. Instinctively, I brought my arm forward and captured his hand in my armpit. I thought I had him. He just dug his fingers deeper into the tender flesh.

Grunting with the effort not to scream and to get those fingers away from me, I reached out and grasped the lamp. I wanted to smash the hard, wooden base on his head, but the angle was wrong. I grabbed what I could, that being the base itself. I swung the lamp over my back and brought it down on his shoulder.

It had little effect other than to have his fingers dig deeper into my pit. Instead of a second swing, I brought the lamp forward and jabbed it directly into the body behind me. I remembered that the bulb was busted and I assumed that the broken glass might cut him enough to get him off me. What I didn't count on was a helping hand I got from the electric current.

There was an audible spark. The broken bulb dug into his arm. He yelped and the fingers in my armpit left. I rolled forward and my legs crashed to the ground. I rolled again to get distance from him. Still holding the lamp, I got to my knees and assumed a fighter's stance. With a short yank, I pulled the cord out of the socket. I flipped my grip on the lamp so I held onto the thinner end and was ready to smash the heavier base on his head.

The guy found his feet and stood to his full height. Crap. He had five, six inches on me. This wasn't going to be easy.

In the light that shafted in through the blinds, I saw his smile and the teeth underneath. The hair was dark and ruffled. The dark short-sleeved shirt was askew and there was a dark line down his arm. Was that blood? I didn't know, but I saw the muscles flex under his skin.

He moved slightly and the light struck the rest of his face.

Amos Peete.

Time to change the equation.

I had an idea Peete might not realize I had unplugged the lamp. The plastic cord might surprise him. Why not give it a go?

I swung the lamp in the air. Peete flinched backwards, but the cord ran across the floor to give him a heads up on its approach. He stuck out a hand and grabbed the cord in midair. With a quick tug, he yanked the lamp out of my hands.

I took that moment, surprised as I was, to change my tactics. I was close enough to my kitchen table that a quick reach landed my hand around the back of one of the chairs. I picked it up, took one step forward, and swung for the fences.

Distracted as he was in dropping the lamp, most of the chair found its mark. The legs crashed into the side of Peete's head and I was happily rewarded with a yelp of pain. He fell to his knees, his hands gripping his head.

Having played baseball with his head, I decided to play football, too. I kicked him. The man was fast. He shot out an arm and deflected my kick. The momentum knocked me on my ass.

"Shit!" I cried. "I'm here for one thing, but I don't have a problem taking something out of your hide."

Enough talk, I thought. I got my feet under me and

ran back to my bedroom. I reached my chest of drawers and found my gun in its leather holster. I cleared it and turned to the door. I cocked the gun and let fly a bullet. It smashed into the door frame. Wood splinters flew into the darkened air. Some of them must have landed in a tender spot because the man in the other room swore. I grinned but my glee faded almost instantly.

"I got more where that came from!" I shouted.

"So do I." A second later, I saw the flash of his gun.

Thankfully, I was in a crouch or else I'd have had a new hole in my head. I heard the bullet sail over me and smash my bedroom window. The shards tumbled down, tinkling onto the windowsill.

With an effort, I kept as quiet as possible. I knew I had only one shot at this. As soon as I fired, Peete would see the flash and get a bead on me. I wasn't going to give him the chance.

I prayed the ringing in my ears would be duplicated in his. I wasn't terribly quiet as I scooched toward my bedroom door, but I wasn't loud either. I just hoped my knees didn't crack. They didn't, but the wooden floor did.

I froze, holding my breath. I flexed my fingers around the grip of my revolver. I waited.

So did he.

I tried something. "The gunshots'll bring the police," I called. "This is my house. You're the intruder."

Peete answered with another gunshot, this one lower, closer to me, closer to where my voice emerged from the darkness.

In response, I all but lay on the floor. I eased my way backwards to the far wall. From there, I ducked down and slithered under my bed. It was an older model, high off the floor. It was a family heirloom, made by my grandfather. I thanked him for making it with enough clearance underneath for storage. I was hoping it would get me out of this little predicament alive.

I got on my elbows, gun in front of me, and edged myself toward the door. I caught a break. The outline of Peete's lower leg was illuminated from behind by the light coming in through the Venetian blind. From his position, however, I knew he'd be able to pinpoint my location as soon as I fired. That meant I needed to make my shot count.

Also, there was another obvious fact. If he got a bead on me, I had nowhere to go. I was pretty much stuck there under the bed.

My ears were getting back to normal. In the distance, I could hear a siren. Part of me wanted Peete to leave and be done with it. Another part of me wanted to maim him and ask a boatload of questions.

I took careful aim. There was only a sliver of leg showing from around the doorjamb. I held my breath and slowly squeezed the trigger.

The gun fired. I heard a yowl of pain from my assailant. The thud on the floor must have meant I hit him pretty well. The chorus of curses followed soon thereafter.

Not wanting to assume anything, I forcefully pushed myself backwards, emerging on the far side of the bed from the door, just in case he decided to charge the room.

Instead, I heard limping, then a heavy, meaty thump on the front door.

I stood, my hands holding my gun out in front of me. I eased to the wall and waited.

Peete grunted, wheezing in and out trying to stem the pain. The next moment, he flung open the door. The doorknob, I would later learn, gouged a hole in my wall.

The sirens were louder now. Still, I didn't dare look around the corner. I enjoyed having my head intact.

I counted to five, then braced myself for the pursuit. I took a couple of deep breaths—were they to be my last?—and moved hard into the open door frame.

Nothing.

There was no sign of Amos Peete. Wait. There was. On the door frame, low, was a dark stain. That would be his blood. Damn. How bad did I hit him that he lost that much blood but was still able to walk out of here?\

One part of my mind told me not bad enough.

The other part was glad he was gone.

CHAPTER SIXTEEN

The police weren't glad . The one siren I had heard had grown to two. The lights of their squad cars strobed off the fronts of the houses along my little street. I bet my neighbors were cursing my name. Gunshots, police cars. What's next? Truth be told, I didn't much like gunshots in my house either.

Like a good citizen, now that I didn't wear the badge, I placed my gun on the kitchen table and held out my hands. I didn't want some jumpy rookie mistaking me for a burglar and putting a new hole in me. I stepped out of my front door and let them all see me.

My house is in the middle of my block. The squad cars stopped, one in front of my house, the other partially into the driveway. From each car's passenger side emerged a patrolman. Each man had his gun drawn.

"You the homeowner?" one of them called to me.

"Yes, sir." Always good to give deferential treatment to anyone holding a gun.

"What happened?"

"Burglar. Broke into my house. I discovered him. We fought. We exchanged gunfire. I got him, in the leg." I pointed to the door frame. "He's pretty badly hurt. I suspect he can't have gone far."

Across the street, one of my neighbors turned on a light and peered out his window. He joined just about every other neighbor that I could see.

"We didn't see any man walking down your street, sir," the patrolman said.

"Y'all see a car?" I said.

"No, sir."

I frowned. How had the gunman gotten away so fast? I nodded to the house. "Might as well come in. Don't need the neighbors looking at everything."

Ten minutes later I was sitting on the couch, ice pack on my head, when Detective Howard Malone strode in my door. He wore a brown suit, wrinkled from sitting at his desk too long, with a solid yellow tie, loosened at the neck. His fedora was dirty and he needed to shave. Some of the men didn't think dressing up for the night shift earned them any bonus points.

I knew Malone from back in my days with the department. Ours was a relationship built on helloes in the hallways and the coffee room. We never worked a case together but he wished me well. And he never held what happened against me.

He took off his hat and held it by the brim. "So you got people shooting at you, Wade. Guess you turned out to be a decent PI after all. If they ain't shooting at you, you ain't doing your job. What was it? Jealous husband?"

"Ironically, I don't rightly know." I gave him a rueful smile.

"Case you're working?"

"Probably."

"Does it have a husband?"

"Yes, but not a jealous one. Has lots of chickens, however."

He cocked an eyebrow. "Chickens?"

"Yep."

He glanced over at the contents on my kitchen table. He tried to read the stacks of paper and notes I had started making since my last case, the one about the Nazis here in Houston. "What's this?"

"Nothing about this shooting." I wished I had had more time to put those things away. I didn't like having to explain my sudden preoccupation on finding Nazi sympathizers here in Houston.

You see, a few weeks ago, after the Lillian Saxton case, a fellow by the name of Dietrich proved to be the culprit. What struck me were his words as he was hauled away in cuffs. "Mr. Wade, you may have arrested me, but I assure you: there are many, many more who share my passions. You can't stop us because you don't even know who we are."

Ever since then, I'd started doing some digging,

maybe to find out if what the Nazi said was true. I hadn't made much progress, but what I had made was lying there on my kitchen table.

"Damn Nazis. I look forward to the day we get in this goddamned war so we can kick Hitler's ass."

"You're sure we're getting in?"

He looked at me like I was from Mars. "Of course we are. It's only a matter of time. The yellow isolationists are doing their damnedest to keep us out of it because they know everything will be changing after that. Ain't no way we can stay out of it, one way or another."

"FDR said America's neutral." I reminded him of the official policy.

"You think Mr. Roosevelt's gonna sit idly by and watch Hitler chew up Europe? Highly unlikely." He shook his head to clear it. "But that's a discussion for a bar, not here in your house." He took out a pad and pencil. "Why don't you tell me the whole story?"

I laid out the gist of the attack, giving him a play-by-play description complete with my walking around the house, showing him angles and positions.

"You know, a man in your line of work ought to keep his gun on him all the time. You never know when a jealous husband might come calling."

After that night, I gave it serious consideration.

I gave Malone all the pertinent details. The police

photographers got all the pertinent images. Eve a couple of newspapermen arrived and got their thread. Would be interesting to see how it plays in the papers the next day. After about an hour, I had my house to myself. The quiet was both ominous and comforting. The ringing in my ears had faded away, but I kept hearing the sound of my own gunfire and the bellowing of the guy I hit him. I knew it was him or me, but I still didn't like shooting a man.

There was a knock on my door. I flinched, then cursed myself for flinching. But seriously, why wouldn't I?

Holding the gun in my grip, I opened the door. Gordon Gardner stood on my porch.

He gave me a funny look, then looked at me from head to foot.

"What are you doing?" I said.

"Looking for the holes. Glad I don't see any new ones."

I invited him in and closed the door behind me. He took one look at the gun in my hand. "Okay, Wade, you can put that away."

I gripped it tighter. "I'm fine. I'm just a little jumpy."

"Understandable." Gardner took off his hat and tossed it on a chair. "I know a remedy for that." He opened his suit and pulled out a flask of whiskey. He shook it and the brown liquid sloshed around. "Got some glasses?"

"Yeah." I trundled off to the kitchen, coming back with a pair of highball glasses and a small bowl of ice. He poured a couple of fingers into each glass, giving me a bit more than him. We lofted the glasses.

"To life," Gardner said.

"To life." I drained half the liquid in one gulp. The whiskey burned my gullet but felt reassuringly great. I collapsed onto the couch that, an hour ago, was nearly my death bed.

Gardner moved his hat and took the chair opposite me. "So, what's the real story?"

I told him everything. He listened carefully. Afterward, he said, "Who the hell would have thought chickens would be worth killing for?"

"It's not the chickens." I ran my fingers over the ice cubes. "It's this." I held up one of the ice cubes. Inside, clearly visible in the cube of frozen water, was the diamond.

"Holy Toledo! Is that real?"

"Absolutely, and definitely worth getting killed for. Or attacked." I pointed to my head.

Gardner gulped down the rest of his whiskey. "So how does that fit in?"

I told him, giving him a chance to refill our glasses.

He whistled under his breath. "I'm not used to

agreeing with Oliver Aldridge because, you know, he's a lying, cheating son of a bitch, but I have to agree with you here. It's his diamond, fair and square. Kruger's just going to have to get over it."

CHAPTER SEVENTEEN

The next morning was rough. My feet hurt, my hands hurt, and my head hurt. I had forgotten to brush my teeth so my mouth felt like cotton and smelled like anything but cotton. The sunlight streaming in through my blinds woke me. I blinked away the night and sat up. I showered with very hot water and loosened my muscles enough to feel human. The cold water rinse helped me wake up. I toweled off and put on fresh clothes. With a new outlook on life, I considered making my own breakfast, but opted for a restaurant. I grabbed my keys and the gem and walked out to Max's Restaurant.

I ordered eggs, bacon, biscuits, and black coffee. As I read the paper and enjoyed the meal. The more I thought about it, the more excited I became. With the diamond in hand, I had all I needed to get Teague to call off the slaughter and save my client's chickens. I chuckled to myself. When you got right down to it, I was working for chickens. Wonder how I should represent that to future clients. Didn't matter. All they would care about were results. And I was getting results.

I paid my tab and drove over to the health inspector's office. I walked in and noticed Danielle and Clara both at their desks. I sauntered up to Clara and nodded to Danielle. "Teague in yet?"

"He is. You want me to tell him you're here?"

"Nah. I like the element of surprise."

Danielle gave me an unreadable look. "You look like you're holding all the cards."

"I am." I grinned and tapped my pocket. "And I even have an ace up my sleeve. The ace that should win my client the lives of his chickens."

The two of them exchanged glances, but I left them wondering. I rounded the desk and made my way back to the health inspector's office. I heard his voice from behind his closed door and stopped to listen before I knocked. Most of the words were muffled. I was far from hearing the entire conversation, but a few words trickled into my ear, a key one being "Kruger."

Wanting to see his face, I let myself in.

Teague turned to me with an angry look. He went ashen when he saw me. He stammered into the phone and then hung up.

"What are you doing in here? You're not allowed, and you're certainly not allowed after what you did yesterday."

"Relax, Teague." I pulled out and lighted a cigarette. "I'm just here to talk."

"You were here to talk yesterday and you wanted me to do something I simply cannot do."

I turned one of his chairs around and leaned on the back of it. "What if I told you the reason you were forced to order the slaughter of those chickens was now gone?"

"I'd say I don't know what you're talking about. We had a legitimate health concern raised in the proper procedure."

I reached into my pocket and plucked out the diamond. I held it up with my index finger and thumb for him to see. The stone caught the light from the overhead bulb and the sun from the window and dazzled.

"This, Mr. Teague, is why you were told to slaughter the chickens. Someone you know lost the diamond in Mr. Smith's chicken pen and wanted to kill each and every one of them to find it. I found it last night. In a pile of chicken shit. Not a fun job, but, then again, it'll save the entire flock."

Teague stared at the diamond, mouth slightly agape.

I snapped my fingers.

He blinked and shook his head. "I've never seen a diamond before," he whispered.

I indicated the ring on his finger. "What, you not spring for one for the wife?"

He smiled wanly. "It's a fake. We can't afford one on a government salary."

Something else clicked into place. "How much were you getting to do this job?"

"Already got two hundred. Was getting three more after the job was done. Seems a pale thing when you consider the price of the diamond."

"Indeed." I pocketed the gem. "Now, about that slaughter order, you cancel it right now and I'll go back to my client and report success."

Teague seemed to shake himself back to reality. "I can't. I mean, it's part of the legal system now."

I narrowed my eyes. "Explain."

"Well, you see, once a complaint is raised, it has to jump through all the hoops. You can't just stop it. Just about anyone can initiate a challenge, but only top governmental people can stop an inspection."

"What do you mean by 'top'?"

He swallowed. "Well, higher up in the pay grade that I am."

"So you're saying you can't just pick up the phone and make a call and cancel the inspection and the slaughter?" My heart was sinking into my stomach.

"No, I can't."

I sighed. What was plan B again? "Tell me one thing at least: what was the name of the man who came to see you the other night?"

"Marlowe."

"Was he the thief or just the messenger?"

"I think he was the thief."

"How'd he blackmail you into ordering the slaughter? What's he got on you?"

Teague sank into his chair and put his head in his hands. "I can't say anything. It's part of the pact one takes when one joins."

I leaned forward, knocking ash into his ashtray. "Join what?"

"I can't say. I won't say. I'm already in enough trouble. Suffice it to say, I'm a member of a group. Or, rather, an informal member. It's a group that looks out for their own, no matter what."

I put two and two together. "And this Marlowe guy is part of the group?"

He nodded.

I frowned. "What kind of group is it?"

He looked up at me, his hands still covering his mouth. "I can't say. It's not allowed. If you're in, you know. If you're out, you don't."

"So, you're telling me Marlowe got you to order the slaughter because you're both part of some secret group?"

"I can't say one way or another."

I sat there, cigarette burning down, thinking about things, what this case had brought to me. I thought about all the people involved, what they had said, what they had done. I ran through the time line in my head until something jarred loose.

"The night Marlowe came here, after hours," I said, stubbing out the cigarette, "Clara worked late. She said Marlowe looked at her funny." I gave Teague as intense a stare as I could muster. "Is Danielle a member of this group?"

His silence told me the answer.

I dashed back into the lobby. A few folks were waiting in line. Clara was helping them, but Danielle was gone.

"Where is she?" I said.

Clara stopped talking with an old woman at her desk. "She said she had to go to the ladies' room."

I sat at Danielle's desk to wait. I gazed at her accouterments: desk pad, typewriter, pencil cup, desk calendar. I looked at all the notes on the calendar, with tasks to do and checkmarks beside most entries. There was one for today: "1:10 p.m. - Meeting." I glanced at my watch. A quarter to ten.

"How often do y'all have meetings?"

"Whenever we need one."

"You having one today?"

"No."

I stared at the entry, mulling the time over in my mind.

I checked my watch. "How long she been in there?"

Clara frowned. "She should have been back by now."

I got up and strode toward the rear of the office building where the restrooms for the employees were situated. I put my ear to the ladies' room door and heard nothing. I knocked softly. No response. Still a little apprehensive, I opened the door. "Hello?"

More silence.

I bent down and looked under the two stalls and saw no legs. Turning, I trotted back to the front lobby. "Where does she live?"

Clara turned to me. "Why? What's wrong?"

"She's gone and I've got to find her. Where does she live?"

"In an apartment over on Vine. Number three ten."

I picked up the phone, then put it down again. I fumbled in my pockets for my notebook. Rapidly, I flipped pages until I found the one I needed. Smiling a little, I picked up the phone again and placed a call.

"Hello?" said the voice on the other end.

"This is Wade, the private detective. I've got a job to do, if you're willing. And you need to bring your gun."

CHAPTER EIGHTEEN

The drive wasn't terrible. I arrived at Danielle's apartment ten minutes later. I stood and waited for about five minutes before someone came out of the complex. I doffed my hat to the young lady and held the gate for her as she left the premises. So trusting. So foolish.

I ascended the stairs, then approached Danielle's room with caution. I wasn't sure what to expect. Walking down the hallway, I hoped my shoes didn't squeak or a floorboard didn't give away my presence.

Putting my ear to her door, I listened. For a few moments, I heard nothing. Then, a shuffling of paper. Next, footsteps doing their best not to sound too loud. I reached into my jacket and verified my gun was secure in its shoulder holster. No need to go in like a cowboy. Perhaps we could just talk.

I reached out and grasped the handle. I gave it a gentle twist. Aha! Movement. Was she expecting someone? Probably, but not me.

Turning the knob all the way, I prayed that the door wouldn't squeak. Carefully, I opened the door keeping my eyes peeled for anything. Through the sliver of space, I could see only the interior of Danielle's room. I opened the door wider and saw the back of a figure hunched over a desk. I opened the door the rest of the way. Without another thought, I threw the door wide. It slammed into the wall.

The person hunched over the desk uttered a short gasp and dropped the sheaf of papers. She turned around and then gaped at me, open mouthed.

"Hello, Danielle. Going somewhere?"

She put a hand over her chest, trying to calm her breathing. "Mr. Wade, you scared me."

"Was it me that scared you or the fact that I wasn't someone else?"

She tried for a smile but it faltered on delivery. "Both, really."

"You were expecting Marlowe? What are y'all planning? A getaway?"

"Well," she stammered.

"Don't bother. Let me ask you a question: if you were in on it, how did you expect to get the real diamond?"

For the first time since I had met her, Danielle Bowie's countenance changed. Gone was the sheepish, slightly flustered girl. In her place was a steely-eyed woman. "Because you were going to bring it to me."

I paused, pondering the meaning of her words. "How do you mean?"

"You found the diamond last night." A knowing smile crept into her features. "I'm just glad it was you and not me digging through all the chicken shit to find it."

Not fully seeing the thread, I decided to bluff. "I don't have the diamond. I think you're mistaken."

"Oh, I know you have it, Mr. Wade. You had it with you when you went to meet Teague an hour ago. You tapped your coat pocket. That's all I needed to know. The only thing left is for you to give it to me."

I cracked a smile. "Even if I did have it, how do you think you'll make me give it to you?"

She reached over to the writing desk. From under a book, she pulled out a snub-nosed revolver. "Because I'll shoot you if you don't."

Having guns pointed at me was becoming a common occurrence as a PI, much more so than when I was a cop. I made my smile widen.

Danielle frowned. "Why are you smiling? I'm willing to shoot you to get the diamond."

"I still have an ace up my sleeve." Over my shoulder, I said. "Now."

Martha Weber came into Danielle's apartment. In her two-handed grip, she held her own revolver aimed squarely at Danielle.

"You always this cavalier with your life, Mr. Wade?" Martha asked.

"Not usually. I just needed Danielle here to confirm

she's in on the heist." I tilted my head at Danielle. "Thanks, by the way." I walked over to Danielle and took the gun from her. I opened the cylinder and dropped all the bullets into my palm. I put the bullets in my pocket and tossed the gun across the room. "Have a seat."

Danielle, wary of Martha's gun which was trained on her, moved over to her couch and sat. "May I light a cigarette?"

"No." I walked over to her and shook out one of my own. I offered it to her and lit it.

"You have trust issues, Mr. Wade," Danielle said.

"I do." I motioned to Martha to pull a chair over and set near Danielle. She complied. Looking around the room, I found Danielle's purse. I brought it over and sat across from her. "Let's see what we have in here that says 1:10 p.m."

I rifled through her purse. The usual assortment of female items. Tucked deep into the bottom was an envelope. I opened it and pulled out three train tickets, all for a coach seat on the 1:10 p.m. train out of Houston at Grand Central Station.

Three? What had I missed?

"Who's the third ticket for?" I said. "You and Marlowe, I get. Who's the third?"

It was her turn to smile. "Wouldn't you like to know?"

I read the names on the tickets. Preston Marlowe,

Danielle Bowie and...

"Amos Peete?" I stared at her in astonishment. "You know Amos Peete?"

Danielle smiled at me and shook her head. "You don't think I'd let my brother stay behind and wind up in jail, do you?"

The revelation was surprising, but what was more surprising was that I didn't have a clue how this all fit together. Danielle and Peete are siblings? In what world did that make sense? She must have been the one who had Peete tail and get to know Clara. See what she knew on the night Marlowe visited Teague. Then I showed up and he started in on me, going so far as attacking me in my own house. It's because he was looking for the diamond, but I gave him enough of a fight that he had to hightail it before the police showed up.

"Marlowe?"

"He and I are lovers, if you must know, Mr. Wade."

Most of the pieces were now falling into place. "Marlowe was hired by Kruger to get the diamond Aldridge bought before Kruger could get it. That means—"I made sure I had my facts somewhat in order—"Kruger and Marlowe are both part of that mysterious organization."

"It's more of an informal society, if you must know."

"And, if Teague isn't a part of the society, that means

Marlowe has something on Teague to force him to order the slaughter. But, if you're Marlowe's lover that means you know about this organization."

Danielle gave me a pitying look. "Mr. Wade, I not only know about the organization, I'm a member of it."

I stood. "Well, then, looks like we have a date at the train station."

"I'm not going anywhere." Danielle blew smoke in my direction. "And Marlowe is an expert thief. He'll smell a rat a mile away if you show up alone."

She was right. I paced the room while Martha continued to hold her gun on Danielle. I looked at the two of them. The thing that had stuck in my craw for a couple of days finally dislodged.

And now I knew how I was going to catch Marlowe.

I raced across the room and picked up the phone. Danielle suddenly looked worried. "Who are you calling?"

"The police. You're going to jail."

Danielle actually laughed at that. "You seem very certain, Mr. Wade."

I spoke into the telephone, then hung up. Walking over to Martha, I motioned for her to stand and I whispered something in her ear.

"Are you sure?"

"Positive. Think you can handle it, seeing as the two of y'all will be alone together?"

For the first time since I'd met her, I saw Martha's smile. "We'll do just fine." She angled a look at me. "This mean I have the job?"

"Absolutely."

"And what are you going to do?" Martha asked.

"I'm going to go see an old friend."

CHAPTER NINETEEN

The University Savings and Loan building was a short, five-story brick structure in the West University district of Houston. Located just off Kirby Drive, it was among the tallest buildings in the area. It had the air of being the biggest fish in a moderately small pond.

Oliver Aldridge was that fish and his savings and loan was the pond. His wealth was probably ill-gotten but his influence was oddly substantial. You'd think that a fish like him would only have influence in the hiring and firing of his employees, but you'd be wrong. He knew people, powerful people. I decided that he owed me a favor.

I parked my car and strolled into the lobby like I owned the place which, for the next few minutes, I did.

A guard noticed me first. He didn't do much other than unfold his arms and hook his thumbs in his belt. I paid him no mind. Instead, I walked straight across the lobby until I reached the receptionist who sat in front of an ornate office. Now, "ornate" by bank standards is several rungs lower on the scale than, say, that of an oil man or a rancher. Still, it was the fanciest office in the room.

I rapped a knuckle on the receptionist's desk. She looked up and then over her glasses. Her brunette hair was beginning to show streaks of gray.

"May I help you?" Her tone indicated that the correct answer was "no."

I pointed at her boss's office door. "I need to see him."

"I'm sorry," she said but didn't mean it. "Mr. Aldridge isn't seeing anyone this morning."

"He'll see me."

"Why?"

I leaned down closer to her ear. "Because I know where the diamond is."

She frowned.

"Just tell him. I promise he'll see me." I waggled my eyebrows and waited for her to comply.

She threw a glance at the security guard. His impassive stare offered her no hope. With another stink eye at me, she rose and walked primly to the frosted glass door and slid inside. The lobby was quiet, but I still couldn't make out the conversation going on in there. Probably helped when the bank had to foreclose on some poor soul.

A few minutes later, the door opened and the receptionist walked out followed by a man who wasn't Aldridge. Turned out it was a bank vice president named Sanderson. He was short and portly. There was almost no hair on his head. His face had the pucker of a man who had just peeled and eaten a lemon. This wasn't going to be good.

Mr. Sanderson didn't offer me his hand. "I'm sorry, but Mr. Aldridge isn't taking any meetings this morning, mister—what is your name?"

"Wade. I'm a private eye. Mr. Aldridge should know me. I visited his wife yesterday, but not in the way you just thought of." I reached into my jacket and pulled out a business card. "This is for you in case you can't remember my name."

The puckered mouth actually shrank more. "No need for name-calling, Mr. Wade."

"I didn't call you a name. Don't say I did." I indicated the card with my chin. "You gonna give that to Aldridge?"

"Probably not," Sanderson said. "But I'll see you out."

I stood my ground. "I'm not sure if your secretary told you, but tell Aldridge I have the diamond." I smiled. "He'll know what I mean."

Mr. Sanderson paused a moment, clearly thinking things over. I helped him out.

"Would you like to be the one to explain to your boss how you knew who had the diamond but then felt it your duty to escort that person out of his grasp? I'm offering myself to you as long as you take me to Aldridge. You'll be a hero. Maybe you can buy some more lemons." I raised my eyebrows.

Sanderson just stared at me. He noticed his secretary

and the guard looking at him.

"I don't think you can just walk in here and demand anything, Mr. Wade."

"Maybe not, but the only way I'm leaving here is by being dragged. Then, won't everyone comment on that? It might even end up in the paper. You think your boss will like that?"

Sanderson pursed his lips and gave a noncommittal shrug. "Wait here." He walked back to his secretary's desk and picked up the phone. He dialed and waited, then spoke in low tones.

To his secretary, I said, "Does he eat lemons for breakfast?"

She looked at me and stifled a chuckle.

Sanderson nodded, then nodded again. He shot a look at me. I knew I was in. I really knew it when Sanderson's shoulders slumped, then rose again. He put the receiver down and came back to stand in front of me.

"You got your wish, Mr. Wade. I hope you know what you're doing. Follow me."

***

Oliver Aldridge's office was about as ostentatious as you could get and still be considered something resembling a work environment. The walls were lined with photos of Aldridge and various celebrities, politicians, and other folks I didn't know. Atop one wall hung the taxidermied head of a ten-point deer. The opposite wall had an African gazelle. The accompanying photo showed Aldridge, decked out in safari gear, kneeling in front of a Jeep with the freshly shot gazelle in the foreground.

I guess he liked his prey best when they were dead.

Sanderson stood politely out of the way. Three men— let's call them guards—dressed in suits stood at the ready. The bulges in their suits told me they were armed. I still got the impression Aldridge wasn't too sure of my story and wanted to make sure to stay out of the range of collateral damage, to keep his suit clean.

The big wing chair behind the massive desk faced the window at the far side of the office. Out of the window, the main area of downtown shone in the morning sunlight. The traffic down on Kirby Drive was moderate, cars moving up and down its lanes. Thick, velvety curtains framed the window. The desk was the typical banker's desk complete with a green lamp, a desk blotter as pristine as you could image, and a few silver pens standing in pen holders. Two black phones were positioned off to one corner of the desk. A third phone sat opposite the pair.

From behind the chair, the voice of Oliver Aldridge slithered out of his mouth. "I think you and I have had some dealings before, Mr. Wade."

I stepped forward. One of his goons tensed. Another

took a step toward me. I felt the hair on the back of my neck rise. "Yes, we did."

"You were a beat cop on the force, if I remember correctly."

"That's right."

"And what was it you called me?"

The memory jolted to the front of my brain. Inwardly I cringed. It was one thing to call a man a lying, thieving son of a bitch to a bunch of fellow officers with one lousy reporter in the room who passed along the compliment to Aldridge. It was quite another to be talking with the man to whom the jab was directed.

I cleared my throat and threw caution to the wind. I wanted something from him and the best way to get it was the direct approach. "I believe it was something along the lines of a lying, thieving son of a bitch."

Aldridge finally swung around in his chair. I hadn't seen the man in person for a few years, but, evidently, time had been good for him. He was tanned to a nice golden hue. His clothes, as always, were starched so heavily you could use them as a notepad. The gaudy rings on his fingers picked up the light. The tie all but glistened in the light of the room.

He smiled at me. It was the smile of a snake. "That's exactly what you said." He gave me a steady look. "Care to repeat it again, this time to my face?"

"Truth be told, Mr. Aldridge, I'd rather not."

"Too yellow to say it to my face?"

"No, more like that's in the past. That's not why I'm here today." I indicated my suit pocket. "Mind if I get a cigarette?"

His goons eyed me but Aldridge nodded. I tapped a cigarette out and put fire to it. The lungful of smoke soothed me.

"I think you know why I'm here, Mr. Aldridge."

He smiled, showing white but crooked teeth. "Why don't you tell me?"

I walked over to a chair opposite his desk and plopped myself in it. "The diamond."

"What diamond?" Aldridge kept his voice even, trying to suppress the surprise in it.

"You know what diamond," I said. "The diamond you bought. The same diamond that was stolen from your house. Now I've got it. Call it my ticket in here to chat with you."

Aldridge wet his lips. I saw the twitches running just under his skin. I suspect not many people talked to him this way.

He folded his hands. "What would you like to talk about?"

"Chickens."

Some of the men behind me chuckled. Even Aldridge tried to keep a grin from showing on his stoic face. "Chickens?"

"That's right, chickens."

"What about chickens?"

"Well, you see, it's like this." I settled in to offer a discourse. Or, at least, a bluff. "I have a client who earns his living by raising chickens. It's his bread and butter like money is to you or investigations are to me. With me so far?"

Aldridge arched an eyebrow in response.

Right. "Something was taken from you, as you well know or we wouldn't be talking."

He looked at me evenly. "I heard you visited my house yesterday. Interviewed my wife. Made kind of a nuisance of yourself. Why were you there?"

So ended the question-and-answer session. Time for only answers. I needed to get back on top of this. "Investigating," I said, buying time. "Putting things together, looking for the reason why someone would want to slaughter a bunch of chickens."

"And did you?"

"I did. You see, the man who stole the diamond from you ended up losing it in the chicken coop of your neighbor, Mr. Smith. The thief, a man named Preston Marlowe, was set to deliver the gem to the man who hired him, but the only way to get the diamond was to kill all the chickens and examine their carcasses one by one until he found the diamond."

Aldridge arched an eyebrow. "Seriously?"

"Seriously. But Marlowe must not have grown up near a farm because he didn't know that all hard objects like stones or diamonds simply pass through the digestive tracts of chickens. He was looking at the wrong end of the birds."

"And you found my diamond?"

"I did."

"Do you have it?"

"I do."

He snapped his fingers. His men started moving toward me.

"Hey, I don't have it with me. I'm not that dumb."

Aldridge chuckled at that. "You're pretty close to that dumb. I can have my boys work it out of you. Have you howling in no time. You'll just give it to me and be begging for your life."

I spread my hands. "Mr. Aldridge, I'm gonna give you the diamond. It's why I'm here."

He stopped, his mouth agape, staring at me. "What?"

"I'm here to let you know I'm perfectly willing to

return what's rightfully yours."

He narrowed his eyes. "But?"

"I'd like to have you to do a favor for me."

"What?"

"Make a phone call."

"A phone call?"

"Yup. To someone who can cancel the death warrant on my client's chickens."

The room was silent for a moment until one of the goons chuckled. In a flash, Aldridge snapped his fingers and jerked his thumb in the man's direction. "Out." The offending man stopped laughing but stood there, as if he didn't really think his boss had just dismissed him.

"Did I not make myself clear? Get the hell out of my office."

The chastened man shuffled out the door.

Aldridge looked at me. "I misunderstood you, Mr. Wade. You are a man of honor."

"Thank you. Now, who do you know in the agriculture department?"

"Whom."

"What?"

"Whom do you know in the agriculture department? Didn't you pass grammar?"

I shrugged. "Not with flying colors. Is there anyone you can call who can pull some strings and get this slaughter order rescinded? Like that fancy word?"

"Not really. I have a degree from the University of Texas. Where did you earn your degree?"

I scowled. "School of hard knocks. It's amazing how much you can learn from the streets."

"Like how to arrest the wrong man?"

I smirked. "No, that takes institutional knowledge."

"Or a few men in the Houston Police Department who know the truth but choose to ignore it for their own gains." He steepled his fingers. "Now, it is my turn to ask you for a question. You mentioned the thief's name. Do you know his client?"

"A man named Kruger."

Aldridge slammed his open palm on his desk so hard everything on the desk jumped an inch. Despite my cool exterior, so did I.

"God damn him," Aldridge bellowed. "I knew it. I knew it!" He stood so abruptly that the chair went flying backward, smashing into the wall.

Sheepishly walking into Aldridge's anger, I said, "Marlowe and Kruger are part of some sort of secret society that has, as a rule, the unquestioning obligation to right the wrongs, perceived or otherwise, done to its members. Based on what I've learned and what I've been able to deduce, Kruger must have thought it a slight that you bought that diamond before he did. Seeing that as a wrong, he contacted Marlowe to steal what Kruger thought was rightfully his."

"It never was his," Aldridge yelled. "I bought it. The diamond belongs to me."

A new thought occurred to me. "How would you like to have a little chat with Marlowe, see what he knows about Kruger?"

Aldridge turned and leveled his gaze on me. "Do you know where he is?"

"No, but I know where he's going to be. And I've already set a plan in motion to get him. If you, um, would like to be in on it, I have an easy way to make sure you get a piece of him."

Aldridge pursed his lips, then came around his desk and sat on the edge. "Explain."

I did.

He nodded. "I'm taking an awful chance with my diamond, Wade. This had better work."

"It will," I said. "And you'll make that call to Austin?"

He put out his hand. I stood and shook it. Our eyes met. There was something akin to respect in his. He nodded once.

"Great," I said. "Now, who has a phone book?"

CHAPTER TWENTY

Houston's Grand Central Station was the Southern Pacific's main line here in town. The station opened in 1934 and most of the new building smell was gone, replaced by exhaust and sweaty people. Fashioned in the Art Deco style so popular in the 1930s, the main central structure was three stories tall. On both sides jutted smaller two-story wings. Sitting atop the roof were the words "Southern Pacific" in red letters that glistened in the noonday sun.

I walked through one of the side doors. Martha had gone in ahead of me to get herself situated. It was twelve thirty. Plenty of time to flush out Marlowe and nab him for the cops or Aldridge.

The main seating areas were inside the larger central room. Not nearly as grand as the stations in New York or Chicago, the Houston main train station was plenty large for the biggest town in Texas. Of course, this being Texas, there were murals on the walls depicting Sam Houston and Stephen F. Austin.

I approached through the west wing of the station and took my position behind a newsstand. Martha, wearing the clothes Danielle had been wearing, including a broad-brimmed hat, read the Post-Dispatch and wore sunglasses. Again, I noted her figure and her natural curves. Perhaps I had been a little too hasty in my judgement of her. She would do just fine as my secretary. The fact that she could use a gun was a bonus.

A few minutes later, a man entered the station. He looked like the man I had seen meet Danielle. He stood, lighting a cigarette, and scanned the room. Seeing Martha dressed as Danielle, he made his way across the semi-crowded waiting area toward her. He bobbed and weaved through all the milling people and sat down next to her. Poor girl. She actually jumped.

Martha put down the newspaper and folded it neatly. Next, she reached up and removed her sunglasses. I couldn't figure out why she was blowing her cover. Marlowe leaned in and said something in her ear. Without speaking, she reached up with her hand and pointed directly at me. Marlowe followed the direction. We made eye contact. A big grin creased his face. He beckoned me. Mute, but fuming, I complied.

While I approached, Marlowe and Martha carried on some sort of conversation. She shook her head twice, then nodded once. He patted her knee in a somewhat reassuring fashion.

"Sit down," he instructed me. "Let's make sure everyone here sees nothing out of the ordinary."

Biting my inner lip in order not to say something wrong, I took the place next to Martha. Marlowe sat next to her.

He reached out his hand. "I suspect you already know my name, but let's get introduced formal, Mr. Wade. My name is Preston Marlowe."

I took his hand and shook it. The tendons and muscles in his hands felt like a vice.

"Your new secretary was just telling me this is her first day on the job. And you have her out in the field, getting caught by someone like me. That's not good. It's your job to protect her, make sure she stays safe in your office.

Martha bristled at that but remained quiet.

"I presume Danielle is in custody," Marlowe said.

"You presume right. And she's talking up a storm."

The shake of his head was dismissive. "Unlikely." He reached over and plucked the purse Martha was holding. Danielle's purse. "The tickets are in here?"

"You seem to know all the answers, Marlowe, but you still don't have what you want." I grinned at him.

He arched an eyebrow at me. "Not yet, but you're going to give me the diamond now."

I barked out a laugh. "Assuming I even have it."

"It would be in your best interests if you did or could procure it in short order."

"Oh yeah, why's that?"

Marlowe looked across the station and back toward

the offices. He nodded. "Take a look."

From behind an open door, the figure of Amos Peete emerged. I had a second or two to ponder why that was supposed to scare me until I realized Peete was holding Clara. Even from this distance, her eyes were wide with terror.

"Now, Mr. Wade, the diamond."

He didn't stick out his hand with an open palm. He just looked at me with an expectant expression, waiting.

I reached into my inner suit pocket.

"No funny business."

"I don't know any jokes." My arm was like rock. I pulled out the small envelope and handed it over to Marlowe. His fingers, long and lithe, took it in the way a spider captures a fly.

With a sly look, he slid the diamond into his palm. The gemstone glittered in the overhead lights. Martha let out a small gasp at the beauty. I resigned myself to losing the diamond. Which meant Aldridge would not make the call I needed to have him make, Smith's chickens would all be slaughtered, and I'd have a very unsatisfied client.

"Tell Peete to release Clara now."

Marlowe stood. "Come with me."

I stayed seated. "Why?"

"Because it's part of the deal." Marlowe's voice was

laced with sudden menace.

I stood. So did Martha.

"Not her."

"She works with me," I said. 'She goes where I go." Not really sure why those words suddenly blurted themselves out of my mouth. Might have been I wanted to have two against two.

Marlowe's shrug was nonchalant. "Have it your way. It's on you if she gets hurt."

He strode across the lobby. Martha was giving me an odd look I couldn't place. I held out my hand, motioning her to go first. She did and I followed.

The three of us arrived at the doorway where Peete was still holding Clara. I got a better look at her face. Yes, she was truly scared, but, then again, I'd be, too, if a man were holding a knife to my side.

"It's okay," I told her. "It'll all be over soon."

Marlowe tsk-tsked. "Wade, you need to figure out who to bring into a case and whom to leave safely back home. This is a far too dangerous business for amateurs, especially female amateurs."

Martha, having had it with Marlowe's offhand comments, jabbed an elbow into his side. He nearly doubled over with the sudden pain.

"That's for thinking so slightly about women." She

spat out the words.

Marlowe rose and glared at her, full-on hatred in his eyes. That's when Peete hauled off and slugged me once in the jaw. The hit knocked me back into the open door. I banged my head and saw stars.

"That's for the other night."

Martha knelt down next to me. For a moment, I couldn't figure out which one of the three images I saw was the real one. A shake of my head cleared it.

"You certainly have a way with people," my new secretary said.

I offered her a lopsided grin. From across the station, the loudspeaker called for boarding of the 1:10 p.m. train. Folks stubbed out cigarettes, folded newspapers, and made their way to the train.

"You don't have your tickets, Marlowe," I said. "What are you going to do now?"

He gave me another pitying look. From inside his coat, he withdrew two tickets. "Use these. You knew I'd have a backup plan, didn't you? You are dense."

I stood and faced him. Instinctively, he took a step back. Straightening up, I tilted my head to look at him down my nose. "Not so dense as you think." I raised my hand and offered him a mocking salute.

With all the folks milling about in the station, the new players in this game weren't immediately obvious.

Slowly, however, as we all looked around, men in suits started moving toward our position. A few wore police uniforms.

Marlowe whirled on me. "You didn't."

I shrugged. "You know me; too dense to know any better."

The train whistled for final boarding. Marlowe looked to his right and the north door. Two uniformed cops stood just outside. Across the station at the south door, two other policemen stood at the ready. And in the middle, moving slowly but steadily toward us, was a small cadre of officers led by none other than Captain Oscar Burman.

Was there a news camera nearby? It was about the only reason Burman would be out in the field. Nevertheless, his clout meant that the boys in blue were taking this seriously.

And why shouldn't they? Oliver Aldridge was involved.

Marlowe turned to Peete. "There a back way through here?" He meant the small room right in front of us.

"Think so. Might get us to the train."

"Blast the train, idiot." Marlowe spat out the words. "We just need to get to the car." He motioned Peete toward the inside of the room. "Let's go." He wheeled. "My turn," he said, walloping me in the gut. I doubled over, but caught his arm in both my hands. Barely breathing, I held on once as he tried to yank his arm free. Another slug to my jaw loosened my grip. I crumpled to the floor.

But I had slowed him down. That was all I wanted. Peete and Marlowe scurried farther into the station's offices, knocking over people who happened to get in their way. I wasn't going to let Marlowe's slugs be the last word. I got to my feet. After a couple of deep breaths, charged after him.

The fleeing pair weren't hard to follow. No, the hard part was getting around all the onlookers who were too busy watching where Peete and Marlowe went even to consider there'd be someone else right behind them. I started hollering, trying to clear the way. It worked well enough.

Peete was a good ten or so feet ahead of Marlowe. He was better at dodging and weaving through the offices and onlookers. But he was no match for the two patrol officers he ran into just as he opened an outer door. True, all three of them tumbled to the ground, but the cops used their bodies and kept Peete pinned to the ground long enough to slap the cuffs on him.

Marlowe saw this in a glance and took a side hallway. A few seconds later, I skittered around the same corner. This hall was lined with various offices on one side and the dispatcher on the other. Charging ahead, I started to gain on Marlowe. It was a stroke of luck that he banged into an outer door and it didn't open right away. That enabled me to close the distance and tackle him. The combined weight of our bodies forced open the door. We both tumbled down a short stairway and sprawled out on the ground. The sun was blinding and the dust that kicked up got in my eyes. I couldn't see Marlowe, but I sensed he was trying to get up. I swung my leg out toward a sound and made contact with someone.

Blinking the dust out of my eyes, I realized I had tripped Marlowe and he lay on his back. The roar of the train's engine starting up drowned out most sounds, but a few choice words escaped Marlowe's lips. I grabbed a handful of dust and threw it at him, but it didn't do any good. I tried to get up, but my ankle gave way as soon as I put weight on it. Must have sprained it. In any other circumstance, that wouldn't be a big deal. But in this one, with a crazy man trying to escape, it was a huge deal, especially when he put his hand in his suit and pulled out a pistol.

"I should shoot you, Wade," Marlowe rasped, "just for the hell of it, but I just don't have the time. But, I can't have you following me either. Remember I have this."

From beyond my vision, another hand appeared. It grasped Marlowe's gun hand at the wrist. His knuckles whitened as the mysterious hand ground down Marlowe's bones. There was an audible pop as something broke. Marlowe screamed and dropped the gun.

It was only then that the body of the man to whom the

hand belonged came into view. Oliver Aldridge. Next to him were a couple of goons. And, from seemingly out of nowhere, police officers and Captain Burman ran up to our location.

"I want the record to show," Aldridge said, "that this man has stolen something from me and I aim to get it back." He said these words, not as though he was asking for permission but as if he were a lawyer in court.

Burman felt obliged to nod, but Aldridge, still with Marlowe's wrist firmly in his grip, was already searching all his pockets. He withdrew the small envelope and let Marlowe's wrist go. The entire arm fell limp. Two patrol cops got the thief to his feet and cuffed him.

Aldridge opened his palm and shook out the diamond. If the thing was brilliant under a lamp, it blazed in the sunlight.

Burman pushed his hat to the back of his head and absently scratched his hairline. Even Marlowe stopped whimpering long enough to marvel at the gem's beauty.

Aldridge spoke first. "I want to thank you, Mr. Wade, for retrieving my stolen property."

I looked up at Burman. "I thought you said there was no crime."

The police captain merely shrugged.

Martha sidled up to me and tried to get me to stand. She had me put my arm around her shoulders. Together, we stood.

"Who's this?" Burman asked, head nodding our way.

"This is my new secretary. Martha Weber, meet Captain Burman. You'll need to know him because he and I have, um, history."

Burman scowled. "You sure you want to start in with this guy? He can be a pain in the ass."

Martha patted my hand. "I'll keep my own counsel, thank you, Captain. But can I get one of your men to help me? Mr. Wade here is rather heavy."

Burman raised his eyebrows, then motioned one of the cops to help me.

In front of the station and around us, a crowd had gathered. From inside the crowd, reporters with notepads and cameras moved forward and began snapping pictures.

Burman turned his back on them, straightened his tie, and put his hat back down firmly on his head. He gave me a wink and turned. He put a hand out to Aldridge meaning for the banker to walk forward and greet the reporters, but Aldridge begged off.

"Mr. Aldridge, sir," Burman said, "would you like to make a statement to the press?"

Aldridge slid the diamond back into the envelope. It disappeared into a pocket. He glanced over at me, then back to Burman. "Yes, Captain, I would." He held up a finger. "But first, I have to make a phone call."

"A phone call?" Burman said, puzzled. "Who do you have to call?"

Aldridge had already started walking back toward the station. "I have to call a friend in Austin about some chickens."

ACKNOWLEDGEMENTS

Back in May 2013, I wrote *Wading Into War*, Benjamin Wade's first story. I went on to write a couple of book featuring a completely different set of characters. Late that year, I wanted to return to the world of 1940 and Benjamin Wade. Thus, *All Chickens Must Die* was born. At the time, I hadn't written *The Phantom Automobiles*, Gordon Gardner's first novel. The ending of that book meant that I had to fix up a few things here in *Chickens*. It proved to be a fun challenge.

The title of *All Chickens Must Die* proved elusive. For the longest time—up to and including when I delivered the manuscript to my editor—I had no title. I can't even say for sure how the phrase "all chickens must die" entered my head, but it did. And it stuck.

Regarding the words, I can write them, but I can't make them shine without the help of my editor, Anna Marie Flusche. As with all my 1940s-era stories, she called me out on a few phrases that were too modern, verified my historical accuracy in other cases, and generally tightened up the prose. Every page had marks, of course, but I always look for the little checkmarks near certain passages. It meant she enjoyed parts that I hope all readers enjoy. As always, any issues with the novel now are all on me.

Thank you again, Anna Marie, for making this a better book.

READER RESPONSE

Thank you, dear reader, for reading *All Chickens Must Die*. I'd love to hear what you thought of the book. Your feedback is important to me and for helping other readers find books they like. In this new age of publishing, word of mouth is just as important as it has always been in spreading the news about good books. Online reviews are a new form of word of mouth.

If you enjoyed this book, I would appreciate you leaving an honest review over at Amazon or any other review site. It really helps other readers find this book.

And if you'd like to know about upcoming titles, please sign up to my mailing list.

OTHER BOOKS BY
SCOTT DENNIS PARKER

WADING INTO WAR
A Detective Benjamin Wade Mystery

Benjamin Wade's first case!

Houston, 1940

Benjamin Wade is a laid back private investigator whose jobs are so mundane that he doesn't even carry a gun. He thought his latest job was going to be easy.

He thought wrong.

Hired by beguiling Lillian Saxton to find a missing reporter with knowledge of her brother's whereabouts in war-torn Europe, Wade follows a lead and knocks on a door. He gets two answers: bullets and a corpse.

Now Wade must unravel the truth about the reporter's death, Lillian's brother, and the whereabouts of a cache of documents that uncovers a shocking story from Nazi-controlled Europe and an even more nefarious secret here at home.

Excerpt:

Chapter One

<u>Monday, April 22, 1940</u>

Even though I was new to this private eye gig, I knew

something wasn't right when I walked up the sidewalk to the front door of 518 Oak Street. It was definitely the house I wanted. The case had taken me that far.

What worried me was the silence.

It was the day after San Jacinto Day here in Houston. It was funny celebrating the anniversary of the victory that won Texas its independence while the Nazis were invading Norway. Everyone thought France might be next. We weren't at war yet, jobs had returned to the city and lots of guys were working. That included me after my stint with the police and my subsequent enforced vacation.

No, what bothered me was the quiet. This was a neighborhood of bungalow houses. Families lived here, families with the husband off working and the mothers staying home with the children. The Depression might have subdued the job market, but it didn't subdue the baby making market. I stood there, sun blazing through my hat, and looked up and down the street. Nothing. No one was out playing in the yard, walking the dog, or planting daffodils in the front flower beds. That's what people did when they weren't working. But that wasn't happening on Oak Street.

Strange. As I looked up at the house, a nice bungalow with tan bricks and a small porch, something in my gut turned over. That kind of feeling had served me well back when I wore a badge, so I listened to it. Still, the leads I had uncovered pointed in this direction. It's what Lillian

Saxton had hired me to do: find Wendell Rosenblatt. He was a journalist who had gone missing a few days after he arrived here in Houston following a stint in Europe covering the war.

This was the kind of job I did: find people. I did the same thing when I wore the badge. I just found it easier with the power of the people behind me. Flying solo as a gumshoe brought with it an uncertainty, one that kept me on edge most of the time. It made me wary, more wary than when I wore the blue uniform.

I stepped up on the porch and listened. Still that strange quiet. Nothing, not even from inside the house. It needed a paint job. Houston's heat and humidity can do a number on exteriors. Mine needed more than just paint.

I rapped my knuckles on the door. Instead of hearing footsteps, I heard something I didn't really expect: gunfire. Bullets slammed the door with dull thuds that splintered the wood. The thick door saved me. Had it been a thin one, like the ones on my house, I would have been thrown back onto the lawn with new holes letting the sun shine into my guts. As it happened, I had time to duck and roll forward. I thought I had done alright, until the bullets smashed the windows right above me and shards of glass rained down. Keeping my head down, I scooted forward to the edge of the porch. Thankfully, the little white railing that fronted the porch didn't extend to the side or else I'd have been trapped.

I slid off the porch and down the short cement steps,

landing on the broken driveway. I won't kid you: I was scared to death. My heart was pounding in my chest and I had to use the house as support while I tried to catch my breath. There wasn't a car under the carport and the side-sliding garage doors were closed.

My ears still rang from the gunshots. It took me a moment to realize the shooting had stopped. Glancing down the street, I still expected to see people coming out of front doors or peering out from behind curtains. No one emerged from any house, but I saw some blinds open. Good. There were witnesses. Always good to have witnesses when the cops show up and start asking the gumshoe pointed questions.

As a rule, I don't pack my gun when I'm doing footwork. I find it best to talk first, let the fists fly second, and lastly, bring out the iron if all else fails. My revolver was in the glove compartment of my car, but I was damn sure not going to run across the open lawn to try to get it. Doing so would put me in the firing sights of the shooter. It might even let him get away.

There was a part of me that just wanted to hunker down where I was, let the shooter retreat and leave me alone. I'd tell Miss Saxton "No, I couldn't find Mr. Rosenblatt at the address given to me by the snitch, thank you very much." I'd just been shot at, so I considered adding to the list of expenses I'd provide her at the end of the case.

But the itch inside my head turned me around. I wasn't yellow, that was for damn sure. I preferred my fights to be as even as possible. I'd lost my share to my cocky mouth, so I had learned to tone it down a bit. Best practices and all. Getting shot at, however, did something to a man, showed his true character. And, there I was, trembling like a little girl while the sounds of footsteps in the house moved to the back.

From across the street, the blinds moved again and I caught a glimpse of white skin against a green dress. I couldn't see the face, but the head was cocked in a way that told me the woman was on the phone. Damn. The police would be coming, sooner than I wanted them to. But I was sure not going to be the shrinking violet Mrs. Green Dress was most likely describing me as right now.

Steeling myself, I got up on my haunches and scooted near the back door. Without my gun, I resorted to clutching the only thing I could find on short notice: the broom leaning against the side of the house. It was so light I knew it'd be nearly useless. You never bring a knife to a gun fight and you sure as hell don't bring a broomstick. Unless you're the Wicked Witch of the West and, well, we know how that one turned out.

I peered around the back of the house. As with the front porch, there were three cement steps leading up to the back door. There were two large windows presumably from a breakfast room facing the back. I couldn't risk moving under them for fear the shooter would spot me and have a clear shot. Above me was a small window, probably the one above the kitchen sink, judging by the sponge resting on the window sill. That left me in a quandary: where would the shooter exit the house? Out the front door risking the eyes of witnesses or out the back? A chain link fence enclosed the entire yard and the detached garage. In the driveway of the backdoor neighbor's house I saw a black sedan. It faced the street, ready to drive away fast. My intuitive gut told me this was the shooter's car.

I needed to end the stand-off. Picking up a few pebbles from the ground, I threw them at the front porch. They rattled around, sounding like boulders in the tense quiet.

The footsteps in the house moved quickly toward my position. The back door flew open and the shooter emerged. With the broomstick, I did the only thing possible: I stuck it out and tripped him.

He flew through the air, arms flailing. Truth be told, he looked pretty funny. He landed face first on the gravel. The impact knocked his hat askew but, surprisingly, he kept a grip on the gun. I sobered up when sunlight glinted off the polished metal of his gun, the barrel aimed directly at my heart.

THE PHANTOM AUTOMOBILES
A Gordon Gardner Investigation

You met him as a co-star in *Wading Into War* and *All Chickens Must Die*. Now, Gordon Gardner stars in his first feature story.

Gordon Gardner, Ace Reporter!

There's not a story he can't crack. He's got his finger on the pulse of his town. His dogged tenacity means no politician is safe. Even the U. S. Army keeps tabs on him to ensure he safely harbors national secrets. And he looks smashing in a tux.

His latest assignment is a basic police blotter piece: a pedestrian struck dead by a car. As a reporter who is second to none, Gardner's disappointed. How could a simple accident be worthy of his considerable talents when there are so many other more interesting stories to cover? Even his pairing with a beautiful photographer doesn't lighten his mood.

His editor wants the piece yesterday. The police already closed the case. But then Gardner asks a simple question: why would a seemingly normal person willingly dive in front of a speeding car? Witnesses said the man went crazy just moments before he leapt to his death. What he alleged made no sense: he said the cars on the street didn't exist and there was only one way to prove it.

He was wrong. Dead wrong.

Now, Gordon Gardner, in defiance of his editor and the police, resolves to investigate the mysterious circumstances behind the dead man's life and uncover the real truth behind the phantom automobiles.

Excerpt:

Chapter One

"I've got two dead bodies," Elijah Levitz, the editor of the Houston Post-Dispatch, said, flipping two pieces of paper between the fingers of each hand, "and I'm gonna let one of my two junior ace reporters pick first."

Gordon Gardner inwardly bristled at the word junior but knew that he'd one day be the senior ace reporter. He stood in the main newsroom with the other reporters and hoped he got first pick. Having successfully flirted with the editor's secretary long enough to get the gists of both stories, Gordon knew which one of the stories would have the privilege of bearing his personal "Gordon Gardner" stamp.

But which one would he get?

When the editor called a meeting, the news hounds had gathered liked sheep to a shepherd around Levitz. The portly man constantly had his necktie loosened, his open collar dirty around the inside ring, and a cigarette hanging from dried lips. The unlit stick bobbed up and down as he spoke and handed out assignments. Each assignment was on a slip of paper torn from a stack held together by an iron rod and a cast iron nut. Levitz claimed it was a piece of the Hindenburg but few believed him although no reporter, copy boy, or secretary ever said so to his face.

When Levitz called out a story and assigned a reporter, that man—they were all men—would plow through the throng and snatch a piece of paper Levitz handed out. Barbara Essary, the editor's secretary, sat at a nearby desk and jotted notes. Sometimes the boys in the newsroom swapped stories. As a rule, Levitz didn't mind the switching except in those times when he reminded his reporters that he was the editor and he assigned the stories as he saw fit.

This was one of those times.

"I think we all know which ones I'm talking about," Levitz continued. "There's the crazy guy who jumped in front of a moving car and lost, and the mugging death of William Silber, local artist. The latter's more of a fancy obit, the former's just a basic crime blotter filler piece."

Gordon looked down a re-read the slip of paper listing the job he already had. A puff piece on the local nightclub owner, Bruno Clavell, who had recently built his first club in Houston after a successful string of similar nightclubs in Dallas, Ft. Worth, San Antonio, and Austin. It didn't amount to much, but he'd certainly get to dust off his tux.

In the stuffy room, not every reporter wore a jacket. Gordon ditched his long ago to the back of his chair next to his brand-new desk near the window. Next to him, Jack Hanson, an older man with three kids and a wife, needed more deodorant. His body odor wafted around him like a fog. Gordon eased away under a false pretense, all the while wondering how Hanson had three kids.

"I'm gonna get that top story," Johnny Flynn said to Gordon. Shorter than Gordon by at least four inches, Johnny nonetheless had an effortless aplomb that surrounded him. His charm and good looks opened a lot of doors and he nearly always had his tie cinched tight. "And I'll get the next promotion by, you know, actually writing something that's true."

Johnny, a rival reporter, still hadn't accepted the fact that Gordon received a promotion for fabricating a news story. To him, you wrote and then you accepted the accolades. What made matters even worse for Gordon was that he couldn't say anything about the nature of the story. For all Johnny knew, Gordon's story was about a bank robbery foiled by the police. The real story involved Nazis in Houston. As a result, he had to suffer Johnny's tirades and oneupmanship.

Gordon hated it. But he loved his desk next to the window so when Johnny got a little too full of himself, Gordon would just saunter over to his desk and stretch out while Johnny had to content himself with a small hovel in the middle of the newsroom.

"Don't talk about stuff you don't know a damn thing about," Gordon whispered. He nodded to their boss.

"Y'all done?" Levitz asked. His cocked eyebrow spoke volumes.

Both junior reporters nodded.

Levitz sniggered. "There'll be no switching. You get what you get and you won't throw a fit."

What was this, kindergarten?

"Harry," Levitz said, "got a dime."

Harry Vinson plunged his hand into his pocket and produced the coin.

"Now, since Johnny here wrote the last big piece for us, I'm gonna let him call it. What's it gonna be, Johnny?"

"Heads," Johnny called out.

Harry flipped the dime in the air, catching it between his open palms. He uncovered and called out, "Tails."

The grin on Gordon's face could've lit up the marquee at the Metropolitan movie house. "I'll take…"

"Not so fast, Gordie," Levitz said, using the nickname Gordon didn't particularly like. "You only get the right to choose the slip of paper. Left hand or right hand."

Again, Gordon thought, is this kindergarten? He wanted the story of the dead artist. Marie Gardner, his mother, taught art in school and was part of the committee that helped found and open Houston's Museum of Fine

Art. Gordon knew he could make William Silber's obit shine.

Being right handed, Gordon's natural tendency was to pick right. But he had been under Levitz's black cloud for a few weeks. Sure, Gordon had successfully bartered his silence for the new desk and promotion, something Levitz had agreed to under pressure. But the editor didn't like his hand being forced and had rewarded Gordon with lesser stories. The last high-profile story Gordon got still only landed on page two. To date, the only page-one story Gordon had was the fake story he had written.

"Left," Gordon said.

"Good choice," Levitz said. "You get the crazy man."

Gordon's pained sigh brought chuckles from the guys around him.

"Johnny, you get Silber," Levitz said. "Alright, boys, let's make some ink."

As the throng started to disperse, Gordon moved against the stream toward Levitz. "Wait, boss," Gordon said, "I'm better for the artist profile. I know more than Johnny does."

Johnny, who remained in place as the reporters and photographers moved past him, just watched.

"Don't care," Levitz said, turning to Barbara and motioning her to follow him. He threw the two pieces of paper in the trash can and sequestered himself in his office.

She gave Gordon a sympathetic look. "Sorry, sweetie." She straightened her skirt and joined Levitz, closing his door.

Gordon shook his head, catching a glimpse of Johnny's grin. Now his was the marque bright one. He turned and sauntered away.

Looking down, Gordon caught a glimpse of the pieces of paper Levitz had just thrown away. Frowning, he fished them both out of the trash. He looked at each of them.

Both pieces of paper were blank.

ULTERIOR OBJECTIVES
A Lillian Saxton Thriller

What if the only way you could discover who killed your brother was to lie to your commanding officer?

May 1940. Western Europe is on edge, wondering when the Nazis will strike. America is neutral, woefully unprepared for war, and President Roosevelt tries to steer the dicey waters of international diplomacy and keep the United States out of the conflict. It is in this environment when Sergeant Lillian Saxton, US Army, receives a cryptic message from an old flame who now lives in Germany: meet in Belgium and he'll not only give her the key to the Nazi codebooks but also information about the man who murdered her brother.

Lillian conducts all her missions with panache and confidence, even when bullets start to fly and enemy agents zero in to kill her. She's more uncertain of how she'll react when she sees the man who broke her heart or how she'll get out of Belgium when the Nazis launch their invasion.

Excerpt:

The door opened a crack. Half a face peered out. Lillian made eye contact and the person's eye widened in surprise. He grunted and tried to close the door quickly. She rammed her shoe in the space and prevented it. Next, she slammed her shoulder into the door. Taking the other person by surprise, she flung the door open, banging him in the face.

Lillian stormed into the room. A distinct odor, a new one, met her. She recognized it but had no time to determine what it was. The man had quickly recovered and was moving towards her.

She recognized him as Brown Suit in the instant before his fist flew at her. It came from her right side. She raised her right arm to deflect the blow while, at the same time, pivoting on her right foot. She used his momentum in her favor. His fist met air and he momentarily lost his balance. That gave her time to crash her left fist on his face.

Years ago, when Lillian had joined the Army, she knew her size and weight would never prevail for long in a fist fight. Lillian felt confident in her abilities if her opponent was a woman. When fighting a man, however, she knew her size and weight meant she needed to end it as quickly as possible. Speed and dexterity were her greatest allies. She knew her blows couldn't end fights with a single thrust, so she honed her ability to rain multiple blows on her opponents.

Her left fist landed on Brown Suit's jaw. She brought her knee up a second later and smashed his chest. Finally, with her right arm now free from deflecting his one swing, she placed her hand on the back of his neck and shoved him downward.

Brown Suit toppled to the floor on his hands and knees. He held his head at such an angle that Lillian knew she had stunned him good. She took a step back to regain a proper fighting stance.

His hand shot out and clipped her ankle. She lost her balance and stumbled backward. She reached out for something to stop her movement and found only air. Lillian backpedaled a few more steps, her thick heels clogging on the wooden floor. A few more feet and she hit the back of a couch. This stopped her backward movement and gave Brown Suit time to stand.

He charged.

Still not quite on perfect balance, Lillian gambled. Brown Suit expected to body slam her. In response, she fell to the floor, landing on her back. A few puffs of air escaped her lungs but she was rewarded by the surprised look on his face as he sailed over her, arms outstretched.

Lillian rolled over and got to her feet. Brown Suit hit the wooden back of the couch and fell to the floor again. A grunt of rage erupted from him but she didn't press him nor did she move closer. His hitting her ankle told her he knew how to fight. Better to get a good handle on her surroundings than to risk another swipe at close quarters swipe.

The interior of the apartment was spare. The couch she had met. Only a coffee table fronted it. The large room had a small kitchen off to her left. A modest wooden table and chairs were to her immediate left. On the far wall was a door that likely led to the bedroom.

Lillian looked around for a weapon. She found none. Not even a plate or a knife on the counter. Only a radio. She judged it too heavy for effective use.

Brown Suit now stood opposite her. His hair had fallen in his face and he swiped at it. A stream of blood coursed from his lip. The red spot left by her fist was already starting to bruise.

"You're an interesting one," he said. "How did we miss you?"

We? Lillian didn't have time to think about that now. She studied his face, watching his eyes and his body for the next move. What she saw took exactly one second to process. It was a subtle change in his expression. A relaxing of his grimace. And a slight shift of his eyes to a spot behind her.

She ducked. In the same moment, she swept her leg out behind her. It met something solid. Another person's leg. She heard a cry of surprise from that person—a man. She hoped her action might give her a precious few seconds to readjust to this new scenario. Two to one. Not good.

The other person lost his balance and fell. He landed almost directly on the seat of one of the kitchen chairs. The momentum and his weight cracked the wood. It gave way and splintered into pieces.

It also gave her a weapon.

She reached out and grasped one of the broken chair legs. Out of the corner of her eye, she noted Brown Suit was reaching his hand into his suit pocket. Chances were good he wasn't trying to be gentlemanly and offer her a tissue.

Holding the chair leg like a baseball bat, she swung. With his hand buried deep in his suit, there was nothing he could do. The wood connected with Brown Suit's face. He crumpled to the floor.

Not waiting a second, Lillian pressed her advantage. The other man was now on his knees. She recognized him as the man reading the newspaper in the lobby. Unfortunately for her, Newspaper Reader had already drawn a pistol and was bringing it to bear on her.

She shifted her grip on the chair leg from a baseball bat to a fencer's grip. She extended her arm and jabbed at the gun hand. Newspaper Reader, having just witnessed Lillian swing with two hands, was momentarily surprised at her action.

He swatted away the chair leg. That was exactly what she had hoped for. She wanted him to think that was her only move.

It wasn't.

Lillian let the shattered chair leg leave her grip. She leapt into the air and brought her leg around in a roundhouse kick. The thick heel of her shoe found its mark. Already on his knees, the man huffed in pain and crashed to the floor.

She landed on both feet. In a single movement, she kicked the pistol across the room. She pivoted and assumed another fighting stance just in case either man had more fight in him.

They didn't.

And that's how Honeywell's men found the situation when they stormed into the room, guns drawn.

ANTHOLOGIES

I have had the honor of placing two stories in two anthologies edited by James Reasoner. I am immensely proud of each story as they enabled me to use my history knowledge and my love of old-fashioned pulp fiction.

TALES FROM THE OTHERVERSE
Edited by James Reasoner

Other times, other places, other stories than the ones we know...These are the Tales From the Otherverse, where anything is possible and things never work out quite the way you'd expect. Some of today's top talents in popular fiction turn their hands to tales of alternate history. Featuring new stories by bestselling, award-winning authors Bill Crider, Lou Antonelli, Scott A. Cupp, Robert E. Vardeman, James Reasoner, and more. Explore the Otherverse and see what might have been!

Excerpt from "The Great Steamer Riot of 1936"

The trumpeter played a total of five minutes without taking a breath before the people in the dance hall realized he was a steamer.

He was a tall, blonde, well-built man who looked like he had Kansas blood coursing through his veins.

The nearest plant to Kansas was the steamer factory in Chicago, along the rail lines. He appeared a wholesome, good old American boy from the plains. That's probably how he got as far as he did.

No one knew how Leo Blake learned to play the trumpet. His was probably programmed him that way. He played it brilliantly. Louis Armstrong may have been the reigning king of the horn, but Leo Blake could've taken Uncle Louie for a ride. That's easy enough to realize considering Blake could literally blow for a full hour before for he'd have to blow off steam.

That was the real trick to being a steamer in the middle of a world full of humans: appearing human while simultaneously not being one of them. Later, when the federal officials swarmed into the local dance hall in North Texas interviewed all the patrons, they all said how normal Blake appeared. Even the dance hall owner, George Frank, believed Blake to be human.

"He wore glasses. The same kind that Sigmund Freud wore. I couldn't tell if the light was reflecting off the lenses or behind his pupils."

The dance hall sat at the edge of the town square in Denton, Texas, a small university town forty-five miles north of Dallas. It was homecoming and George Frank, alumnus of North Texas Teachers' College, had arranged to bring Rip Howard's Fiery Fifteen big band to town for the big homecoming dance. Howard traveled the southern circuit of dance halls and was a big hit down in Houston and New Orleans.

The hall itself was modest: a two-story building, wood-paneled walls, and a small stage at the north end. The refreshment table sat in the rear of the hall, next to the kitchen. Chairs lined the walls and groups of youngsters, in twos and threes, huddled together. The sheriff was there, mostly as a father, since his daughter was a senior that year, the prettiest girl in the school. He didn't want any of the boys to manhandle her the way the crowd eventually manhandled the steamers.

WEIRD MENACE: Volume 1
Edited by James Reasoner

The Weird Menace pulps flourished for less than a decade, from the mid-1930s to the early '40s, but while they were popular, they delivered adventure, excitement, and spine-tingling thrills in quantities rarely seen before or since. Mad scientists, deranged henchmen, damsels in distress, and stalwart heroes raced through their pages in breathless, over-the-top, never-ending action. A good Weird Menace yarn really is just one damned thing after another.

Rough Edges Press asked some of today's best authors of popular fiction to write Weird Menace stories, and they delivered. Settle back and let us spin a few yarns for you.

But keep an eye out behind you. You never know when something might be sneaking up on you.

Excerpt from "The Curse of the Monster Makers!"

Dexter Tremane slammed the stolen car into third gear and rounded a hairpin turn on the old country road. The rear caught gravel and fishtailed, threatening to send the machine into the nearby ditch. That wasn't what Dexter needed. What he needed was to get as far away as possible from the pursuing patrol cars.

He risked a glance back. Off in the distance, through thick woods and country brush, red and blue lights pierced the darkness. They were many. He was one. He had the advantage of speed and knowing where he was going. They had the overwhelming numbers. And, he reminded himself, he was woefully outgunned.

He pressed his foot harder on the gas pedal. There was no more he could do. He willed the car to go faster. It didn't comply.

The road was dirt. All the cops had to do was follow the dust that billowed up from the car's wheels. The lightning that streaked the sky threatened rain. Dexter turned his willpower to the heavens.

They laughed at him.

In a flash of lightning, he saw something up ahead. Was it the turnoff to the rendezvous? It was a small, thinner dirt road, nearly hidden by the sagebrush and mesquite trees.

He slowed and risked a quick illumination of his headlights. He threw the car into a sharp turn and something inside the engine gave way. The clanging sound deafened his ears and all but called out to the cops.

"Blast!" he cried. His fists were like iron grips on the steering wheel. He fought for control. The car skittered sideways then gained some more forward momentum. It didn't last. The car plunged into the shallow gorge next to the road. The headlights shattered as did Dexter's forehead on the steering wheel.

He must have blacked out for a few moments because the next thing he knew, he woke up coughing from all the dust. He fumbled in his jacket for the box of matches. He struck one and the small flame revealed his predicament. The car had crashed headlong into the gorge and now spanned the small trough. Behind him, the cops had turned their sirens back on. They were getting closer.

Dexter opened the glove compartment and rummaged around to see if there was anything he could use. The owner must have been a Spartan because the only thing inside was a map, a small Bible, and a blunt pencil and notepad. He would have killed for a flashlight.

He pulled the key out of the ignition, got out and opened the trunk. The starlight, while bright, didn't illuminate the interior of the trunk so he lit another match. A gust of wind blew it out almost immediately but not before he saw the tire iron. He closed his strong fingers around the cool metal and hefted it. If push came to shove, he wasn't going down without a fight.

Thing was, he wasn't going down.

ABOUT THE AUTHOR

Scott Dennis Parker lives and works in his native Houston, Texas. He is the Saturday columnist at DoSomeDamage.com. He is the founder of Quadrant Fiction Studio, an independent publisher that specializes in stories that will amaze, excite, and, most importantly, entertain you.

Official author website and blog:
scottdennisparker.com

Twitter: https://twitter.com/sdparker7

Official author page on Facebook:
www.facebook.com/scottdennisparker

Email: scott@scottdennisparker.com

Monthly Newsletter

Sign up for the monthly Scott Dennis Parker email newsletter to receive exclusive sneak peeks at upcoming titles, behind-the-scenes of the book making process, and more.

Plus, you can get a free copy of *Wading Into War: A Detective Benjamin Wade Mystery*. Sign up at the official author website.

WESTERNS BY S. D. PARKER

You've got a lot of choices in what you read. So do I.

That's why I specialize in Western stories that will amaze, excite, and, most importantly, Entertain You.

I call it Old-Fashioned Escapism for the 21st Century.

The westerns I write, under the pen name of S. D. Parker, draw their inspiration from classic novelists from Louis L'amour, Luke Short, and Bradford Scott to modern authors like James Reasoner, Robert J. Randisi, and Peter Brandvold. Classic television shows like The Wild Wild West, Maverick, and The Adventures of Brisco County, Jr. also spur the imagination.

The Box Maker
A Triple Action Western

"The Box Maker" nominated for the 2016 Western Fictioneers Peacemaker Award for Short Fiction.

Emory Duvall practices his simple carpentry trade, knows everyone in town, and stays out of trouble. But when a young gunslinger pulls iron on him and makes an unusual request, trouble lands in Duvall's lap.

Now, the carpenter must figure out how to avoid getting shot...and how many coffins he will have to make.

This exciting new Western from S. D. Parker will have you asking a simple question: what would you do in Emory's position?

Excerpt:

"I make boxes," Emory Duvall said. His hands, held above his head, shook in his sleeves. The small, round glasses, having slid down his nose on account of the sweat pouring off his forehead, perched precariously. You got the impression a good strong wind might just come by and knock them off, landing in the sandy ground of Main Street.

"I know you make boxes," the stranger said. He switched his gun to his left hand and wiped the palm of his right on his pants. "What I asked is do you make boxes you could put a man in?" He glanced around, looking to see if there were prying eyes spying on them. Seeing none, he gripped the pistol with his newly dried right hand and wiped his left.

Duvall gulped, his Adam's apple bobbing up and down over the bandana wrapped around his neck. "I can build any size box you want, mister." He scrunched his nose, trying to keep his lenses on his face. The movement caused whatever friction holding them on to fail. His glasses fell to the ground.

Squinting with the sudden blurriness of his sight, Duvall indicated the glasses. "May I?"

The stranger paused. The midday sun bore down on

the pair. "Look, if I put away my iron, you gon' to run or holler?"

For the first time since the stranger arrived at his shop, Duvall smiled. "Mister, I can't run further than five feet without my spectacles." He said the word 'can't' by adding an extra 'i' in the middle. "But if you want me to build you a box of any size, I'm gonna need my glasses."

The stranger narrowed his eyes. "No funny business, you hear?"

"Mister," Duvall said, "I don't even wear a gun." He tilted his head down to indicate his waist. Other than a thick leather belt of tools dangling from his hips, there was no sign of a gun. His denim pants were stained dark with sweat. Even under the thatched awning of his cutting area just outside his shop, it was nearly a hundred degrees and getting hotter by the minute.

The stranger nodded and, when Duvall didn't move, he said, "All right." He took a step back, giving himself a better line of sight toward the heart of town. As Duvall crouched down and felt for his glasses, the man said, "Tell you what, box man. I'm a'gonna holster my piece, so's we can talk, man to man. But don't be fooled. I can draw faster'en anybody you know. You try anything, even a call for help, and that's the last thing you'll ever say." With that, the stranger slid his Colt revolver back into the holster.

Duvall found his glasses and wiped the dust off of them with part of the bandana hanging around his neck. He replaced the lenses and got a better look at the stranger.

Judging by stubble, Duvall guessed the man to be in his early twenties. The man's face had scars that appeared to be self-inflicted while shaving. The young man's clothes were road dusty and disheveled, sweat staining his arm pits, his stomach, and along the thigh where the holster rested. The hat atop the man's head used to be sharper, cleaner, but had seen much better days. Judging by the way the hat rested on the man's ears, Duvall thought the inner head band must've worn off.

Smiling at the stranger, Duvall said, "You got a name?"

Put off by Duvall's informality, the man said, "Ain't you scared a'me?"

"Mister, I make boxes, but I also make coffins. A man who makes coffins sees a lot of dead folk. Those dead people get dead any number of ways. Bullets and violence are only part of it. You startled me a few minutes ago, that's all."

He started patting his shirt to dry off his hands. The action caused the stranger to flinch and reach for his gun. Duvall stopped in mid wipe, his smile dropping. "I ain't going to try anything. I just want you to know that." Still, his hands shook and he gripped his shirt to try to hide that fact. "Now, again, you got a name?"

The man relaxed and stood straighter. "Murray."

"Duvall. I'd shake your hand, but mine's a bit dirty."

Murray extended his hand. "Mine's dirty, too."

The two men shook hands, the sweat sliding between their palms.

"Now," Duvall said, "you mentioned something about a box, a coffin I assume by your asking. Why do you need a coffin?"

Murray scrunched up his face. "Why do you think I need a coffin? I need to put a man in it." He chewed his bottom lip with teeth that hadn't seen a toothbrush in many a day.

Duvall chuckled a bit. "I know that, Mr. Murray. But I need to know who it's for. You know, for the measurements and such."

Glancing this way and that, his eyes staying an inordinate amount of time down toward the heart of town, Murray said, "It's for me."

The Agony of Love
A Triple Action Western

What would you do if your wife cheated on you with a dandy of a gambler?

John Hardwick answered that question for himself. Now, he's about to act on it.

John Hardwick loves his wife like a Shakespeare sonnet: full, complete, and without equal. Unfortunately, John now finds himself in the crucible of infidelity. He knows the other man's name: Alton Raines, a professional gambler.

John is a good man, not prone to violence, but the images in his mind's eye—of his wife in Raines's bed—puts murder in his heart and a gun in his hand.

Excerpt:

John Hardwick loved his wife Mary like a Shakespeare sonnet: full and complete and without equal. He would memorize the Bard's sonnets as well as the poems of Byron, Blake, and Browning and recite them to her over dinner or in front of the fire in their little home. Their life was hard—he a farmer, she a farmer's wife—but he loved it more and more each day. Even when the hardships of farm life took their toll on him physically, he still loved his beautiful Mary. When the farm life robbed her of her ability to bear children, he still loved her.

But even the surest of love could be tested in the crucible of infidelity. John Hardwick found himself in that crucible now as he stared across the saloon at Alton Raines, his head full of things that normally never entered his mind. Images of violence, hatred, and murder boiled his blood. He wondered how loud the shot would be if he stuck his pistol up against Raines's body and pulled the trigger.

Still, he had to gather his courage. It had taken him over an hour of waiting, drinking, and watching to figure out which patron of the Oak Tree Saloon was Alton Raines . He had asked a couple of men if they knew the. They did, and had easily pointed him out.

Raines turned out to be the dandy sitting at the poker table. His dark hair, slicked back and coiffed perfectly. The mustache neatly trimmed. His suit, gray and adorned with a shimmery purple vest. The black tie formed a perfect knot over a pressed white shirt. Occasionally Raines would check the time on his shiny gold pocket watch. He presented himself in a suave manner, smiling at everyone in the room. Ladies would drape themselves across his shoulders.

All in all, the sight made John Hardwick's stomach turn. It also brought a tear to his eye. He wasn't much to look at. He knew that. Long days of sun and wind and hard work had aged him. He looked ten years older than his age of thirty. His eyes had developed permanent crow's feet. His hands looked like an old man's. And his shoulders sagged a bit, even when he wasn't carrying heavy equipment or hay bales.

He caught a glimpse of himself in the mirror behind the bar and felt an utter dislike for what he saw. Also in the reflection was Raines. It appeared that the two of them were side-by-side. Any doubt as to the idea of what he was about to do vanished in an instant.

John turned and sauntered over to the poker table. There was an empty seat now since a skinny blonde man stormed off in a huff after losing all his money. "Mind if I sit in?"

The remaining men seated at the table stared up at him. Raines sat opposite the empty chair. On the left was a burly red-headed brute of a man. When he held the cards, they looked like playthings in his oversized fists. To the right was a man he knew: Christopher Allen, the owner of the local tannery. The smell of the chemicals on his clothes wafted up and tickled John's nose.

"I don't have a problem with it," Allen said. "Paul?"

The red-headed man downed the last of his beer. He wiped his mouth with the collar of his shirt and shook his head no. He raised the empty mug and signaled for another.

"Alton?"

All eyes turned to Raines. The dandy took his time answering. John felt like he was a prize hog being inspected for quality.

"Can you pay?"

John Hardwick nodded. "Yes, I can."

Raines gestured to the empty chair. "Then by all means, have a seat."

John pulled the chair out and sat. It was a good thing, too, since his legs had begun to shake. The closer he got to going through with what he needed to do, the more nervous he became. The hard leather of his holster thunked on the wooden chair and he had to adjust his posture to accommodate.

A barmaid brought Paul's mug of beer and set it in front of him. He leered lecherously at her exposed cleavage. He mumbled something John found inappropriate and he felt it his duty to save her.

"Ma'am," John said, "might I have a beer as well?" He turned to Allen. "You want one?"

"Whiskey's fine with me."

John faced Raines. "How about you, Alton?"

"It's Mr. Raines. I'm fine." His voice was a smooth baritone, the kind of voice that belonged in a choir or behind a pulpit, and not in this den of sin.

The barmaid left and Raines began to shuffle the cards. "How much you in for?"

John reached into his jacket pocket and withdrew a wad of cash. Allen's eyes widened in surprise. "Tarnation, John. That's a lot of money. Where in the world did ya get it all?"

Where indeed? John had discovered the love letter written by another man tucked discretely into a book of poems he had given his wife on their fourth anniversary. The letter was full of affectionate sentiments that made John cry. At first, he felt the emotional punch in his gut. Then lost his lunch. Mary Hardwick had been out of the house for the afternoon so she was spared John's immediate wrath. In the afternoon hours of that day, as he toiled under the broiling sun, he thought about what to do. What to say.

In the end, he said and did nothing. He planned. He intended to take his husbandly revenge out on the man who signed his name "Alton Raines."

John considered himself a humble man, not too book smart, but he knew how to read and write. And he had the patience of Job. Two more letters had mysteriously arrived at the house. He found both. One of them had the name of the Oak Tree Saloon, the home base for Alton Raines, a professional gambler. On any given night, Raines was there to take the money from unsuspecting folks and fools with money passing through on the trains.

John knew he needed substantial amounts of cash to

join a game with Alton Raines. He and Mary had saved up quite a bit over the eight years of their marriage.

John took it all. He didn't mind. He may lose it to Raines, but when the gambler was dead, John would merely take the money back.

"Inheritance," John lied. "Mary's uncle died. She's the oldest of her family. Left it all to her."

Chris frowned, probably trying to remember if he or his wife had heard this news. John didn't give him a chance to remember. "I'm in. What's the ante?"

"Two dollars. Five card draw." Raines finished shuffling and passed the deck to his left. "Christopher, you deal first."

Christopher took the cards, cut the deck, and threw in his ante. The other players anted up and the game was on.

Mosaic Law
A Junction City Western

What would you do if your spouse was murdered?

Isabella Gilmour woke one morning thinking it was just another day. It wasn't. It was the day the horrifying news thundered down on her: her husband had been shot dead by Bart Conway, the scion of the biggest cattle rancher of Junction City, Texas. In her moment of anguish, she invokes Mosaic Law: an eye for an eye, a life for a life. She makes a simple request of her father: "Go get Stephen's rifle."

Her desperate father begs her to let the legal system work.

Will she, or will she let justice come in the form of a bullet?

Excerpt:

When Isabella Gilmour saw Dick Darby riding at full speed over the rise, she knew something bad had happened. No one rides like that to deliver good news. She stopped her work with her family's horses and waited.

Her father, Malachi Metcalf, heard the hoofbeats as well. He had been working at repairing a section of the pasture fence. He also stopped and leaned against the new fence.

"Expecting anything?" he asked.

"Nothing good," she replied. She wiped her hands on the apron she always wore when she worked.

The rider craned his neck, scanning the area. Isabella wanted to wave her hand and signal Darby, get whatever he's got to say out as soon as possible, but knew that he'd find her eventually. The summer weather here in south Texas scorched the earth. It was August and only crazy people worked outside in this heat. Crazy people or folks that had no other choice to make a living.

Darby spotted the pair and turned his horse towards them. He angled the chestnut gelding around the main house, past the barn, and into the area between the pasture and the hog pen. He barely reigned the horse to a halt before he dismounted. Momentum carried him forward and he tripped, landing face first in the dirt.

"Take it easy, there," Malachi said. "We're not going anywhere."

Darby stood and brushed off his clothes. His shirt, wet with sweat, stuck to his chest. The dirt that found its way there started congealed to mud. He stepped forward and removed his hat.

Isabella's stomach dropped to her feet. Dread coursed through her.

"Mrs. Gilmour, ma'am," Darby began, "there's been an accident."

"What happened?" Isabella said. Her voice croaked with worry and curiosity. Darby was a hired hand on the Gilmour family farm. He mainly worked the fields with her husband. "Where's Stephen?"

"Mrs. Gilmour, I'm sorry to say this, but your husband's been shot dead."

Isabella Gilmour's legs gave out from under her. She slumped to the ground, dust curling around her. She put a hand to her mouth. Tears welled in her eyes.

Malachi crouched next to his daughter and hugged her tightly. The two of them sat there, in the dirt, and cried together. Darby merely stood there, working the brim of his hat, discreetly looking elsewhere. His horse had meandered over near the pasture fence where he and the Gilmour's mares snuffed at each other. He walked over to his mount and pulled down the canteen hung around the saddle horn. He gulped warm water that soothed his dry throat but didn't fill the hole in his heart.

Finally, Isabella looked up at him, her eyes rimmed with red. "What happened?"

Darby wiped his mouth with the back of his hand. He hung

the canteen back on the saddle and neared Isabella and her father. They were both standing now.

"It's a little unclear."

"Dick, you were working with Stephen over the rise on our east property. How can you not know?"

Darby cleared his throat. "Well, you see, I wasn't there when it happened."

"Where were you?"

"I was taking care of nature's call." He sounded sheepish, almost like a child. "I didn't want to do it on your land and all so I went up a ways and took care of my business. It was in the trees. I heard some shouting and hollering. I couldn't hear what was said, but I heard "This is my land" very clearly. It was Stephen that said it."

Malachi said, "Do you know who he was talkin' to?"

"Didn't see his face, but I saw his horse. Gray roan, I believe."

Isabella's face hardened. "There's only one man I know of who rides a gray horse."

"Why'd Bart Conway want to shoot Stephen?" Malachi asked.

Bart Conway was the scion of Bartholomew Conway. The elder Conway moved into the area twenty years ago and generated a bountiful crop the first year. He withstood the droughts that crashed fellow growers' land by shifting to cattle ranching. He really made his killing when the railroad proposed running new track in the middle of his land. He sold his acres for a hefty profit, enabling him to expand his cattle business. The younger Conway, growing up privileged, generally did whatever he wanted, including troublemaking, and his father always backed him up.

Darby had no response. Isabella started walking to the stable. She viciously wiped new tears from her eyes. Minutes later, astride her horse, a beautiful chestnut paint, she said to Darby, "Show me the place."

"Wait a minute," Malachi said. "I'm coming, too."

***

The three riders crested a small rise and gazed down into a small, flat plain. Mesquite trees bordered the far sides and a rocky outcropping framed the north end. Below, the open farm land was almost completely tilled. At the far side, a mule stood, attached to a hoe. On the ground behind the tiller was a body.

"No, no, no," Isabella cried. She dug her heels into her horse's sides. The steed leapt forward and galloped toward the fallen man. Darby and Malachi held back and allowed her extra time to grieve.

Isabella's eye took in the panorama through eyes glazed with tears. She and Stephen had met thirteen years ago. He was new to town, moved here with his parents as an thirteen-year-old. It was an awkward time for him. Schooling back in his home state of Louisiana hadn't been regular. He preferred to work the land anyway. But his parents insisted he get caught up on school and that placed him with Isabella and her existing classmates. They had made fun of the tall, gangly boy who talked funny. Isabella thought it charming, different than the slang she heard every day of her life. She and Stephen had become friends, then more than friends, then husband

and wife. Her classmates stopped making fun of him after he matured and his body took on hard, lean muscles as a result of working the land. The women of the town grew to envy Isabella. The men in town envied Stephen, for Isabella herself had grown into a beauty as well. Two pretty people had found each other in the awkward stage of life and had stuck together.

Now, they were torn asunder.

Openly crying, Isabella jumped off her horse and ran to Stephen's body. The bullet that had pierced his heart left a ragged hole in his work shirt. It was wet with his blood and sweat. She sagged to her knees and cradled his upper body in her arms. She caressed his face and wiped his hair to the side, the way he always styled it for Sunday services. His face had lost the rigor and had sagged into a natural state. He looked like he was sleeping.

Isabella wailed.

After a time—she didn't know how long; time seemed to stop for her—a shadow fell across her and her dead husband. She looked up, blinking in the sunlight. Her father stood nearby. Darby as well. Both men held their hats in their hands. Tears filled her father's eyes.

"Daddy," Isabella said, her voice taking on a distant tone, "go get Stephen's rifle."

A Father's Justice
A Junction City Western

A man shouldn't outlive his son. Neither should his killer.

In a searing new western from author S. D. Parker, you will discover all a father will endure to see justice done right by his murdered son.

Luke Russell was a cowpuncher, making an honest way in the world at one of the biggest ranches outside of Junction City. But he got himself in trouble over a girl, and he paid the ultimate price.

Now, a stranger's in town, asking after Pete Davidson, the man who put a bullet in Luke Russell's gut. This stranger is old, and folks realize it's Luke father, come to kill Davidson. The gunslinger is young and vibrant, just like Luke Russell was. The old man doesn't stand a chance.

Or does he?

The answer comes in a brand-new western written in the style of Robert Vaughn, Louis L'Amour, and Chet Cunningham.

Excerpt:

Chapter 1

"I'm lookin' for Pete Davidson." The stranger's voice was old, aged with smoke, and hardened by time out on the range.

Hector knew Davidson. Everyone in town did. Hector only wondered what fresh hell Davidson had cooked up to get another man to come looking for him.

To the stranger, Hector said, "He ain't here."

"I can see that."

Slowly, the stranger walked to the bar. His peripheral vision took in both the back room of the saloon and the front window. Outside, passersby went about the business of Junction City. The courthouse lawn was free of people on this Saturday afternoon. The Gilmour children walked with their mother across the street, a rangy dog followed them. The clip-clop of hooves and a squeaky wagon wheel pierced the stillness of a late summer's afternoon.

The stranger reached the bar and leaned on it. "Can I get a beer, please?" He reached into his pocket and pulled out a coin. He laid it on the wood pockmarked with knife marks and carvings.

Hector retrieved a fresh glass and filled it. He slid the coin into his hands and stepped back, putting his butt against the far wall. "Why're you looking for Pete?"

The stranger removed his hat and set it on the bar. His matted hair was predominantly gray. What color remained was brown.

"That's between me and him." He downed half the brew in a single gulp. He wiped his mouth with the back of his hand and stared at himself in the mirror behind the bar.

Hector had the impression the stranger had forgotten all about him. It wasn't until Hector fidgeted that the stranger again took notice of him.

"You ever know you have to do something but don't know if you've got it in you?" the stranger asked.

Hector was used to men talking to him, giving up their secrets. But that was from men he knew. "I reckon."

The stranger shook his head. "Bet you have more than one cuss saying something like this?"

Hector nodded. He spoke when he realized the stranger wasn't looking at him. "Yes."

The stranger took another swallow. He drew his attention to the bar top and the gouges in it. Knife cuts and initials coated most of the surface. Some men carved their entire names. The stranger traced his hands over one name, his fingers caressing each letter of the name. His beer forgotten, he studied each of the names carved into the wood.

Hector said, "A few boys carved their names into the wood. I used to get after them, made them fix up what they did. But as you can see"—he indicated a place nearer him—"the fix looks worse'n the carvin'. Pretty soon, I kinda liked having the names in the wood. Became kinda like a rite of passage. New man in town ain't accepted into town lessen' he puts his name on my bar."

The stranger wasn't listening. He went up one side of the bar then returned to his spot. He moved his beer glass and started reading the names and initials on the other side of the bar.

His fingers stopped on a name. A little gasp of recognition escaped his lips.

Hector moved to see the name that had stopped the stranger. "Luke." Hector's blood froze in his veins. He remembered the man who belonged to that name. He remembered how he died.

Realization dawned on Hector. "You kin to Luke?"

The stranger didn't answer. "You knew him?"

"A little." Hector shrugged. "He was new in town,

got shown the ropes by the other cow punchers up on the Alistair ranch. He was a little wet behind the ears, but he learned fast."

The stranger kept staring at the name. "How did he die?"

Hector hesitated. "Look, mister, I don't…"

"How did he die?" the stranger repeated, this time in a forceful voice.

The Killing of Lars Fulton
A Junction City Western

An ambush leaves an innocent man dead and the sheriff behind bars, branded a murderer.

In an exciting new Junction City western from author S. D. Parker, Sheriff Walt Eason finds himself accused of murder, and only Deputy Diego Lange can save him.

Rustlers have stolen heads of cattle from all the biggest ranches in Junction City, Texas, including Bartholomew Conway, the nemesis of Sheriff Eason and his deputies. But when the lawmen open fire on a suspected owlhoot, the dead man is not a thief, but one of Conway's own ranch hands.

Now, Junction City's richest citizen has all he needs to get rid of Eason...at the end of a hangman's noose. Eason's fate falls to his junior deputy, Diego Lange, a half-breed with few friends in town. Lange has only hours to uncover the truth about Lars Fulton and the strange thing discovered in the corpse's pocket or Junction City will have a new sheriff, one who doesn't look too kindly on Diego Lange.

If you like action-packed tales in the tradition of Robert Vaughn, Paul L. Thompson, or Frank Leslie, you'll enjoy "The Killing of Lars Fulton," the first novel-length tale in the Saga of Junction City.

Excerpt:

"I'm not sure I can do it," Deputy Diego Lange whispered. He crouched on a small rock outcropping overlooking the land outside of Junction City. The air was warm, even an hour toward midnight. The new moon cast no glow on the land below. Overhead, the stars sparkled in the night, the constellations mingling among themselves. The heat of the day was giving up its last fingers and succumbing to the cool night air. The smell of sage and hot rock still tickled Diego's nose and those of his companions.

Sheriff Walt Eason grinned in the night. "It ain't no big thing."

"It's no big thing for you, Sheriff," Diego whispered back. "You do it all the time. Hell, you've already started doing it seeing as how the election's coming up. I ain't," he searched for the right word, "as accomplished as you."

Off to Diego's right, he heard a soft snort from Jack Moore. "If I was standing up for my brother, I'd be so drunk by the wedding it didn't matter what I said." Moore was the senior deputy among Eason's rank of three. Typically, he didn't let anyone forget that he was second only to the sheriff. Even tonight, as the three of them hunkered down to catch some cattle rustlers, he made sure to get the catbird seat on the outcropping. He claimed he had eyes like an eagle's and could see clearly in the night. Diego knew that Eason tolerated Moore and acquiesced. But Diego was still irritated that Moore decided to stick his nose into business that was his.

Eason inhaled deeply and let out the air slowly. "When it comes down to it, all you have to do is speak from the heart. It's your brother's wedding. He asked you to stand up for him. Sure, that usually means you gotta give a toast of some sort. Everyone will be looking at you, making you feel puny as an ant. Put all that stuff away. Just remember, this is your brother. Other than your parents, you know him best. All you have to do is…" He stopped and held up a hand. "Quiet."

"I heard him, too," Moore said.

All three men laid flat on the rock their eyes overlooking the grazing area. The dark husks of cattle gently stomping their feet could not dampen the sound of footfalls on the dirt.

Someone was coming.

Down a ways, just to the other side of the cattle, they all spied the distinctive silhouette of a man. He wore no spurs so the only sound he made was the gentle clomp of his boots. He wore a hat so the lawman couldn't make out his face. But they all saw what he was doing: making his way toward the cattle.

In a low voice, Eason whispered, "Remember we have to catch him in the act. Before that, he's just a man out on the midnight walk."

Diego understood. He began to breathe more shallowly, his mind telling him even his breath would give away their position. Moore, on the other hand, fidgeted in his position.

"Don't move," Eason commanded.

The shadowy figure made his way along the perimeter of the group of cattle. Curiously, he reached out a hand and touched the romp of each cow.

Diego frowned. "What is he doing?"

Eason shushed him. "Wait and see."

The man continued to walk around the perimeter. If he kept going that way, he would get perilously close to where the lawmen had stashed their horses. If he found the horses, all bets were off.

That seemed to be the thinking of Deputy Moore as well. "He's gonna find the horses," he hissed.

"Let him," Eason said. "It means we have the element of surprise."

"Why don't we surprise them right now," Moore said. He moved. Small pebbles dislodged and tumbled down the outcropping.

The shadowed man heard and turned toward the sound. He drew his gun and aimed, the barrel swiveling back and forth, not sure from where the sound came..

The lawmen already had their guns in hand. Under earlier orders from Eason, they held their fire. Besides, even with starlight, they couldn't get a direct bead on the shadowed man's location. But when the man opened fire at them, the blossom of flame from his muzzle would give them all the pinpoint direction.

A lead slug pinged near Diego's face. He reacted without thinking. He pulled the trigger of his gun. Moore did the same. Eason held back. Gouts of fire poured out from the barrels of their revolvers. The shadowed figure fell in a clump.

"Dammit!" Eason said. "I said hold fire until he did something." He sighed, sending plumes of dust in the air. He holstered his weapon and got to his feet. "Come on."

Diego felt chastened by his mistake. He had reacted without thinking. Typically that was a good trait for a lawman to possess. But he was still learning. Sheriff Eason, to his mind, was the best teacher in the world. Now Diego had disappointed him.

Eason, Diego, and Moore trundled down the outcropping and approached the shadowed figure. Not knowing if they had killed him or not, they approached from three different angles. The two deputies still held their guns. Eason approached unarmed.

The downed man law sprawled on the ground. His gun hand was empty. Eason kicked the pistol out of reach just in case. The dark patch under the man was likley blood. The more Diego looked at the patch, the larger the patch got. It was blood alright, seeping out of the wounded man and being soaked up by the dry ground.

Eason reached into a pocket and flicked a lucifer

match to life with his thumbnail. He crouched down and brought the light closer to the dead man's face.

"Oh no."

The Naked Con
A Triple Action Western

What do you do when you see a naked man cowering behind a rock?

You'll get the answer in an exciting new western from author S. D. Parker, inspired by the TV show Maverick, the movie Butch Cassidy and the Sundance Kid, and the novels of Robert Vaughn and James Reasoner.

It's not every day that the passengers of a stagecoach in the Old West see a naked man hiding behind a rock. But the motley group of people on a stage bound for Uvalde, Texas, stop and question Finnegan McCall, naked as the day of his birth. He says he is the new manager at the bank in town and a thief stole all his clothes.

But if Finnegan McCall is telling the truth, then who is the stranger at the bank claiming he is the new bank manager?

And why is this stranger asking the assistant manager to open the safe?

This exciting new Western from S. D. Parker will have you who is whom and what it all means.

CALVIN CARTER, RAILROAD DETECTIVE

An exciting new western hero from author S. D. Parker in the tradition of The Wild Wild West, Maverick, and The Adventures of Brisco County, Jr.

The Old West teemed with dogged, badge-totting lawmen, vile, murderous desperadoes, and honest citizens who craved a simple, peaceful life.

Calvin Carter was none of those.

Combine Artemus Gordon's acting ability, James West's panache, Bret Maverick's charm, and Brisco County, Jr.'s unabashed zeal for the adventurous life and you get Calvin Carter.

A former actor who became a railroad detective after tracking down his father's killer, Calvin savors his exciting life, the mysterious cases assigned to him, and the beautiful women he encounters along the way. Together with his partner, Thomas Jackson, Calvin Carter aims to make a name for himself in the annals of the Old West…with flair.

So if you like your western heroes with a little more flamboyance and your stories a bit taller than usual, then you'll love the adventures of Calvin Carter.

The Poker Payout
A Calvin Carter Western

Calvin Carter goes undercover to uncover a nefarious

bribery scam. As always, he deploys a bit of theater when he confronts the owlhoot responsible for murder…with predictably disastrous results.

Excerpt:

Calvin Carter sat at the poker table and smiled. It had taken him awhile, studying the movements of the dealer and the other men around the table, but he finally figured out how they all were cheating. The deck was marked. That much was clear. He, however, didn't have time to figure out what the markings were. Percy Johns was too busy winning another pile of chips.

"What are you smiling at, Carter?" the man across the table asked.

Carter fingered his tie and made his smile bigger. "I just can't get over how lucky Johns here is."

"It ain't luck," Johns growled, throwing a menacing look Carter's way. Johns's suit was rumpled and his tie askew, owing to his constant fiddling with it on his winning streak. "It's all skill."

"Oh, it's skill alright." Carter cocked eyebrows. "But I'm not sure it's yours."

The man across the table paused in the act of raising his highball glass to his lips. The light of the oil lamps overhead glistened on his shiny cufflinks. Slowly, he lowered the glass, the whiskey still swilling in the glass. "What are you implying, Mr. Carter?"

Carter held up his hands, palms out. "Absolutely

nothing, Mr. Tobias. I was merely noting that every man here at this table has a certain degree of skill at this game. Sometimes, a man's skill at poker can win him more hands than the cards indicate. Other times, a man can falter, no matter how good he is." He patted his chest. "My skill just seems to be lacking here tonight and Mr. Johns is the benefactor."

A small crowd had gathered around the table as Johns racked up his winnings. A game of chance had sprouted among the onlookers, seeing as there wasn't going to be a vacancy at the table for the time being. With each successive hand, money and coin exchanged hands, to the choruses of cheers and grunts. A few of the working ladies hung on the arms of some of the men. Despite their earnest entreaties, none of the men would leave.

Jeffery Tobias drained his glass and held it up over his shoulder. One of the dark-suited men directly behind him took the glass and waded the crowd to the bar. With a last, long look at Carter, he said, "Well, Mr. Johns, I don't care what Mr. Carter thinks about his own lack of skill, you're playing a mighty fine round of poker. If I count your chips correctly, your winnings are rapidly advancing on a little bonus."

"Bonus?" Johns said, lacing his voice with extra curiosity.

As a trained actor, Carter felt the massive urge to give Johns acting lessons. Nonetheless, Carter smiled to himself. Things he had suspected were coming to pass.

Tobias sucked in his cheeks as he took a lungful of

smoke from his cigar. He let the smoke waft upward as he spoke. "Yes, Mr. Johns. A bonus. Any man who earns four hundred dollars at the table is entitled to a room with one of my ladies." He paused and smirked. "Free of charge."

Johns actually blushed and Carter fought the urge to roll his eyes.

"Let's get on with the next hand," Peter McKay said. He sat to Carter's left. He was a bearded man and had sweated through his clothes, clogging the smoky air with his stink. Absently, McKay wiped his forehead with the back of his hand. It made a wet sound.

Carter sniggered, "You must like losing more than I do, McKay."

"Shut up," McKay said. To the dealer, he said, "Deal."

Anderson, the dealer, looked at Tobias who nodded. The cards began flying across the table. Carter kept his cards face down, pulling up the corners to determine what he had. As usual, it was junk. He examined his small pile of chips in front of him. He might be able to stretch his presence at the table for a round or two more but, after that, he would have to leave.

Time to force the issue. But first, he was going to have some fun.

The Mark of the Impostor
A Calvin Carter Western

Detective Calvin Carter disguises himself as a French

nobleman to thwart an act of treason that could overturn the balance of power on the high seas. He enlists aid from Evelyn Paige, his former lover and sometimes partner. Carter and Paige have the perfect plan, but when his quarry exposes Carter's lie, it'll take all the detective's unique abilities to avoid a bullet in the gut...to say nothing of stopping the escaping traitors!

Excerpt:

"I can't believe I let you talk me into this," Evelyn Paige said.

"Relax," Calvin Carter said, "it'll all turn out fine."

"Like the time-with-the-saloon-madame fine, the I'm-sorry-Evelyn-but-I-need-a-loan fine, or the I-just-stole-your-case fine?"

"Neither," Carter said. "This is entirely different."

"I swear, Carter, if I didn't need your help with this case, I would never have agreed to this little facade of yours."

"Listen, what we do is dangerous. What's so wrong with doing it with a bit of flair?"

"Flair?" Evelyn said. "That's what you call this?" She shook her head. "What could possibly go wrong?"

"Quiet," Carter said. "Time to talk French."

***

The Alexandria Palace Casino in Austin, Texas, was

one of the most famous gambling establishments in the west. Located just down the street from the capital, the Alexandria was a high-end casino in the vein of the Barbary Coast outside San Francisco or the fancier casinos in New Orleans. Built by Bernard Jameson and named after his wife, the Alexandria was a destination for gamblers, politicians, mercenaries, thieves, and cowboys, sometimes all in the same person. A gambler, it could be said, wasn't truly a professional gambler until he won or lost money in the Alexandria.

The interior was wide, spacious, and gaudy. The namesake woman fancied herself a worldly woman so she insisted her husband decorate in any style that tickled her fancy. Naturally, that led to a hodge podge look and feel, but everything inside was of the highest price.

Perhaps the most famous event at the Alexandria was the all-region poker tournament held each year on the first weekend of May before the heat drove all but the most hardy citizens to the safety and coolness of Barton Springs. If you weren't a true professional gambler if you hadn't won at the Alexandria, you certainly weren't worth your weight in salt if you hadn't at least participated in the tournament.

The evening's crowds were loud and boisterous. The men had dressed for the evening in their finest tuxedos despite the ebbing of the day's heat. The ladies were adorned with the best dresses and jewelry that the city of Austin could afford, and more than a little that it could not. Imported jewelry lined the necks of many a woman, the ones accompanied by men and those looking for men.

It was into this atmosphere that a small gasp by the assembled throng was heard when Pierre Trudeau St. Bontaventure appeared at the top of the balcony overlooking the people on the ground floor. According to the papers, the French aristocrat was making his way across America, recreating and renewing the journey Alexis de Tocqueville made in the United States in the 1830s. He was hoping to find the heart of America after the War Between the States and wanted to find out how much the country had changed since the end of the conflict. Bontaventure had met with the President, the members of Congress, and many of the millionaires in New York and Boston. Now, in the spring, he was railroading across the South on his way to California for the summer.

A fan of games of chance, Bontaventure had picked up the basics of poker along the way and had made his intention known that he would like to join in the tournament. The Alexandria's owner, Jameson, was more than delighted to have such a high-class entrant in his newly formed contest and jumped at the chance.

Half of the Texans in attendance were there not really to participate in the tournament but just to see Bontaventure. The rich and famous were rare in this part of the country, but the Frenchman made up for it just by his presence.

He stood at the railing, gazing at the people like a king to his subjects. He smiled down, loving the attention.

The audience smiled up, loving being loved by him.

On his arm was his translator and confidant, Emmanuelle Gabrielle Leblanc. Resplendent in a white gown, her raven hair was pulled back to reveal her ears and the dangling gold earrings that sparkled in the lights. She had her hand through Bontaventure's cocked arm, but she stood slightly behind him.

In heavily accented English, Bontaventure said, "I want to thank each and every one of you for your most gracious welcome. I have learned much from your country. I have eaten well, I have met many fascinating people, and I have learned how to lose money in poker."

The audience chuckled appropriately. Bontaventure smiled even more broadly than before.

"I look forward to the contest, and I hope not to lose too much of my money." More polite laughter filtered throughout the casino.

Bontaventure leaned over to Emmanuelle and whispered in perfect English, "How was that?"

Without breaking her smile, Emmanuelle said, "Carter, next time, I get the lead and you get the supporting role. I can't stand being your little woman."

"Evelyn," Carter muttered back, "you wound me. Take the dagger from my heart."

"That's not where I'd put the dagger," Evelyn said, raising her eyebrows.

www.ingramcontent.com/pod-product-compliance
Lightning Source LLC
Chambersburg PA
CBHW070822120626
46556CB00002B/628